# All Of These Kids Are Going To Die

## D E McCluskey

All Of These Kids Are Going To Die
Copyright © 2023 by D E McCluskey Ltd.



ISBN 978-1-914381-33-1

Dammaged Productions
www.dammaged.com

**This book is dedicated to all the lads ...**
My mates who have been there with me
through thick and thin, for almost 40 years
Vinny, Dexter, Dell, Stuart, Joey, Lee, Matty, The Morleys (all of
them), Toe Mac, Macca M, Paddy O, Timmy, Carl, Darren,
and all the others who are just too many to mention.
Not one of them will read this book!

# PROLOGUE

He had literally just seen her stab the girl and drag her towards the house. He cursed himself for not being brave enough or strong enough in character to shout out, to startle the attacker and maybe save his friend's life.

But he hadn't been.

When the moment of truth came, he chose the well-worn way of the chicken.

He couldn't understand why *he* hadn't been taken yet. He'd witnessed every single murder, seen it happen with his own two eyes, in real time and in glorious technicolour. His brain and body were confused. He didn't know when he'd last had any real sleep, as every time he dropped off, everything came back to this place and to his friends.

A shiver ran down his spine when he thought about the house; it brought involuntary spasms and the rising of goosebumps up and down his arms.

How could this have happened? How could a person change from being a normal, everyday girl into a ruthless and savage serial killer, hunting down everyone they knew and loved?

The old Windsor place was at the heart of it. He knew this. It's malevolence loomed over everything. Even though it was still night, its shadow radiated evil. Its brooding eyes searched for him, hungry for more victims. Somehow, he knew the house was commanding her, ordering her to perform these atrocities, as she wasn't the type to do them herself. He knew this better than anyone.

Tonight was going to be the night he stopped it.

The night he stopped … *her.*

He gripped the shaft of the hammer so tight it made his hands sweat. He hoped it was more to do with the warmth of the air than the weight of the tool, as he didn't want to hesitate to use it if it was necessary.

With a determined breath, he continued on towards the old property.

He pulled the hole in the chicken wire fence apart and was in the yard of the dreaded place. Within the clutches of whatever evil languished here. He could feel it. It prickled his skin as if some unseen force watched over him, sizing him up as a hungry diner might look at a plate of steak and fries. He was another potential victim, perhaps the last piece of whatever nefarious jigsaw puzzle it was putting together.

He gripped the hammer again, mostly for comfort, and continued towards his final destination.

He had watched every one of them. They had been his friends; they had been *her* friends. He couldn't believe her capable of doing something like this.

Holding back, watching as she disappeared through the dark entrance, he pondered on what was happening. This had been the strangest and the worst Halloween night of his life. *Has it only been one night?* It was a question he genuinely couldn't answer. There had been so much senseless loss, so much violence, so much strangeness. Right now, there was no time to dwell on it, there was too much to do if he was going to bring this whole sorry mess to an end.

And he was determined to end it.

Quickening his pace, he made it to the wooden steps, being careful not to make any excessive noise. He slowed as the house's shadow swallowed him. It wanted him here; it welcomed him. He felt like it had been expecting him, waiting. The door creaked as the wind tugged at its rusty hinges. It was an invite; it was wooing him, lulling him inside with the promise of fun. Glee for the house yet death for everyone else. He toyed with the idea of turning around, of going home and pulling his blankets over his head and forgetting about this whole ordeal.

That wouldn't happen; it couldn't happen, even if he wanted it to. Things had gotten so far out of control. What had started out as a stupid Halloween adventure had rapidly turned into something else entirely.

Something bloody and petrifying.

On entering the house, he knew exactly where he was meant to go.

His throat was dry. The taste of dust, mould, and his own dehydrated breath almost made him gag. He swallowed dryly and continued on his mission.

She was there, just as he knew she'd be.

Almost as if it was orchestrated.

'Bradley?' she whispered, grinning.

## 1.

'I'M NOT GOING in there,' he protested. 'It's haunted. People died in there. They went in and never came out again. Remember the twins from a few years ago?'

'Bradley, there were no twins. It's an urban myth.' Avril was laughing as they sat in Bradley's room playing the latest vampire computer game, where the object was to clear your castle of marauding gypsies before the sun came up and turned you into dust. Avril was good at it, mostly, to Bradley's chagrin.

'A what?' he asked as he turned a big-boss gypsy into a vamp.

'A myth. It's not true. There was no Halloween prank, no dare, and there's no ghosts in the house that killed them.'

'Well, all I know is I don't know anyone who's spent the night in there before,' he replied, exiting the game.

'Well, that's all going to change. We're going in. You'll be the one to miss out. Everyone will be talking about this for years, and you'll be the only one not able to boast about being in there. Besides, I was thinking about me and you, you know, spending Halloween together in a cosy little haunted house.'

Bradley blushed. She knew exactly how to push his buttons. 'I—erm!' he stuttered.

She eased herself out of the beanbag and tossed her game controller onto his lap. 'Come on. It'll be a scream.

There'll be six of us. We're meeting just before it gets dark. There's a hole in the fence we can use to get onto the property.'

'What about security?' Bradley asked, powering down the games console.

'What about it? There hasn't been a security car up there for years.' She shrugged.

He sighed, almost defeated. 'Who else is going?'

'Heather's going.' She sang this as if to tease him. 'I know you like her.' She laughed.

'I don't,' he protested, scrunching his nose. 'She's way too intense.'

Avril raised her eyebrows and continued to laugh.

'Well, there's Ted, Chris, Samantha …'

'Samantha?' Bradley asked, his voice raising at least three octaves. 'Seriously? She's a real bitch.'

Avril chuffed. 'I know. It's going to be epic.'

'I don't know. When is it?'

'Halloween. We'll finish school and go straight there.' Avril was putting her jacket on, getting ready to leave for the short walk home before it got too late.

'Seriously, Halloween? Can't we just dress up like vampires and stalk the neighbours for candy?'

Avril shook her head. 'We're not twelve anymore, Bradley.'

He sighed again. 'Let me think about it. I want to go, but …'

'But what?' she asked, looking at him. 'But you're too chicken?'

'No,' he spat. 'I've just got …'

'Got what, Bradley? I'm your best friend, and I'm going. So, unless you have a secret double life you're not telling anyone about, you'll be home, alone, beating your meat to big-boobed victims in your slasher movie collection.'

He cringed at that and felt his face turn red. *How does she know I do that?* he asked himself. He shook his head before realising she was only jerking his chain. He wished she was jerking something else. He admonished himself for that thought, even though he knew exactly what he'd be doing in ten minutes.

'Well, think about it because it's going to be awesome.' She gave him a kiss on the cheek and left his bedroom.

Bradley was left alone, his cheek still tingling from her swift embrace and his mind already made up. He would be going to the house. Hell or high water couldn't stop him now, not after that little kiss.

## 2.

BRADLEY REGARDED THE steps of the old house. The night was darker than usual, the heavy, ominous clouds filtering out any of the silvery light that the almost-full Halloween moon might have shed. With his trusted flashlight gripped in one moist hand, he stepped onto the old wooden decking. It groaned under his weight. Only it didn't sound like the wood protesting his offensive intrusion, as he might have expected; it sounded like a dying patient on one of those cheesy hospital dramas his mother loved so much.

It sounded fake, theatrical, and grossly overacted.

He swallowed, trying his very best to lubricate the dryness of his mouth, hoping to get moisture into his tubes so if he needed to, he could scream at the top of his lungs.

*Only if I need to*, he reiterated to himself.

He turned back to the yard and saw the rest of the gang. They were watching him climb the steps, each of them grinning from ear to ear. It looked like they were all in on the best joke anyone had played in years. Everyone, that was, except Avril. She looked concerned, scared. She looked like she didn't want him to do what he was about to do.

Bradley raised his flashlight to wave at the group. They all waved back, urging him enthusiastically on. His eyes lingered on Avril a little longer than they should. *I'll be back in an hour*, he sent telepathically. *Wait for me* ... This made him smile as he turned to stare into the gaping maw of the doorway to the old mansion. The darkness inside was intense, all consuming, and hungry.

Folklore stated it was haunted by the spirits of twins, Joe and Flo. He chuffed at the names. *Who calls their twins rhyming names?* The tale was that the twins were new in town, and for a dare, they agreed to spend Halloween night in this house. They went in, there were plenty of witnesses to that fact, probably more than there was in reality; however, they never came out again.

Ever.

The police were called. The house was searched from top to bottom, but they were never found, not even their bodies. Talk of a kidnapper was popular for a while, but no ransom was ever sent, not that their family was rich or anything. Then there was talk of a transient serial killer laying low in the house. Then there were whispers of a dark spirit that had taken them in an attempt to break its own otherworldly contract. It killed them and forced *them* to haunt the house while it shook itself of its tether to this realm and passed on.

Bradley shivered.

He would rather face a serial killer than Joe and Flo, even though he knew deep down they didn't exist.

As he entered the darkness, his mind instantly went to every single horror film he'd ever watched and every book he'd ever read. They all started out this very same way. A stupid teen—or a buxom wench, depending on the era— entered willingly into a stupid situation. The audience knew what was about to happen, yet the protagonist didn't.

It was all good fun … until *you* became the protagonist.

He turned one last time just before giving himself over completely to the house.

There was no one there. They'd either left or were out of his narrow line of sight. He hoped it was the latter. Either way, it unnerved him. He was now alone, totally, and completely.

*Why the fuck did I agree to this?*

The flashlight cut a narrow swathe through the gloom. Dust motes, millions of them, danced in the beam that illuminated whatever it touched and very little else. There were no shadows, no grey areas. If it was within the beam, it was lit; if it wasn't, it was left to his own morbid curiosity and overactive imagination to conjure things that were not there.

He closed his eyes and breathed. He needed to eradicate the visons of monsters, ghosts, serial killers, his mother …

The thought of his mom being in this house scared him more than anything else. He wiped his nose with his sleeve and opened his eyes.

They were there …

Joe and Flo.

Two scared looking kids just a little younger than he was.

Their flesh was pale, their eyes too bright in the beam of the flashlight. Thick, fresh blood dripped from their open mouths. It looked like strawberry jelly drooling from their chins.

Bradley opened his mouth to scream, but nothing came out. The only sound he made was a thin, muffled cry.

He couldn't move. He needed the toilet—his reeling head reasoned it would be a number one *and* a number two.

As one, the twins moved. They raised their hands from their small, emaciated bodies. Dust and dirt fell from their coloured hooded jackets, one red and one yellow, the same tops they'd famously worn on that fateful Halloween night all those years ago.

Their mouths opened wide, revealing dangerous teeth, too many for such small spaces. Each tooth was sharp, dangerous. The thick, dark blood continued to drip as they shuffled towards him.

*Are they floating?*

Bradley turned, needing to get away from the ghastly scene to allow his chest to fill with sweet, refreshing air that would allow him to scream the unholy mercy he had welling up in his chest.

A cold hand touched him.

His flesh froze where it touched.

Another hand grabbed him by the neck. Sharp nails, or claws, cut through his coat. He could feel something tearing, burning into his flesh …

~~~~

'Sweetheart, you're dreaming.'

Bradley opened his eyes. The gloom of his bedroom was momentarily the old mansion. The hand grabbing him was cold and strong. There was malice in the embrace; he could feel it. He jerked from the grasp and rolled out of bed, landing on his face, on the floor. It was only the deep pile rug that stopped his nose from breaking and allowing his own thick strawberry jam to pour from it.

'Bradley, what's the matter with you?'

He recognised the voice but couldn't believe that she, of all people, would be in this house, waiting for him, collaborating with Joe and Flo. It was his very worst nightmare coming true.

'Mum?' he asked, his voice muffled from being stuffed full of carpet.

'Who else were you expecting? Bloody Mary?'

He couldn't tell her that he had been, or someone very much like her.
~~~~

'You were dreaming, loudly,' she snapped. 'I thought I'd come and wake you before I heard things a mother should never hear from her son.'

'Very funny,' he mumbled, easing himself up from the floor, removing carpet fluff from his mouth.

'Aren't you supposed to be doing that house thing tonight?' his mother asked, retreating from the bedside.

'How do you know about that?'

'I'm a mother. I know things.' She laughed, leaving the room. 'Besides, it's Halloween, and crazy kids like you are always doing stupid things on Halloween night. Now come down and get something to eat. We don't want you chickening out, do we? And running home at three in the morning to get some cheese toast, like when you used to sneak into our room pretending you were hungry when we all knew you were just scared.'

Bradley followed his mother down the stairs and into the kitchen.

'Did you ever do a dare in the old mansion?' he asked as they sat around the breakfast table. His father was working, and his sister was at her boyfriend's apartment, as she was most nights. So it was just the two of them. He preferred it that way.

'The old Windsor place?'

Bradley nodded as he pulled a plate filled of scrambled eggs with sausage and mushrooms—his favourite—closer.

His mother blew a raspberry. 'Nope! Absolutely not. Not after what happened to Joe—'

'And Flo,' he finished. 'I know the stories. I just thought you might have—'

'Known them?' It was her turn to finish the sentence. 'Listen, kiddo, I might be old, but I'm not *that* old. That story was being told when I was your age.'

'Did anyone ever live in that house?'

His mother shrugged as she tucked into her own meal. 'Probably. It was built in colonial times.' She looked at her son, who was staring blankly back at her. She shook her head and half closed her eyes. 'That was when the British still ruled this country and we were a colony. Jesus, are these schools teaching you anything these days?'

Bradley pulled a face as he turned his attention to his breakfast.

'That house has always just kind of been there. It's always been *haunted*, but because of Joe and Flo, no one has ever gone in. I remember your father wanted to once, but your grandpa wouldn't let him.'

Bradley chuffed. He'd been flirting with putting the stunt off, but hearing that even his old man was too chicken to spend the night in there made his mind up for him. He was going in and was going to spend the whole night looking out for Avril. He was going to be her hero and come away from there with her as his girlfriend.

That was now the plan, and he was going to stick to it.

Getting up from the table, he went to walk out of the kitchen.

'Excuse me,' his mother shouted, snapping him from the daydream of protecting Avril—and maybe getting a little more than a friendly kiss on the cheek for his troubles.

'What?' he asked, annoyed at being brought back to Earth with a bump.

She pointed at the sink. 'Dishes. If you want my permission to spend Halloween in a spooky house with Avril, then you need to consider that the ghosts of Joe and Flo won't be coming here and doing the washing up.'

He rolled his eyes but grinned as he made his way to the sink and poured hot water into the basin.

## 3.

THE NIGHT WAS mild. It was late October, and it would usually be mild until just after Halloween. Bradley was making his way through town. He'd wanted to stop at Avril's and walk with her to the house, but she'd said something about the girls meeting up beforehand for a milkshake and some Dutch courage.

He had his jacket tied around his waist, as his mom had told him it would get cold in the dead of night. He'd wished she hadn't used the word *dead*, but he'd brought the jacket just in case Avril might need something, or someone, to warm her up in the small hours. He'd shrugged his mother's embrace off after she said this, but deep down, he'd listened, and the jacket went on. His backpack was filled with sugary treats, a cell phone power bank, sandwiches, batteries for his flashlight—as he'd watched every movie where the flashlight batteries ran out at exactly the wrong time. Also hidden in a secret pocket, he had a trusty pack of condoms. He'd wondered if they were past their use by date now. He'd bought them so long ago but had forgotten to check. He didn't think he was going to need them anyway, but just like the Boy Scouts, he wanted to be prepared.

The warm wind whipped through his hair as he walked. His stomach was churning, and he couldn't shake the odd, disturbing feeling that was wracking his body. He wanted to turn back, to cry off sick, to stay at home and hope Avril would be OK. He stopped walking, turned, and looked at the path he'd taken from his house. It would be so easy to just go home, condoms in his backpack or not.

'Bad Brad,' a voice called out to him.

It made him jump.

'Bradders, I didn't think you were coming. Avril messaged and said you might have chickened out.'

It was Chris. Bradley sighed internally. He liked Chris, but the boy was at least six-foot tall already and had more than a hint of what his mother would call *the Brad Pitts* about him.

This meant he was a good-looking kid filled with personality.

'Avril messaged you?'

'Yeah, man. We were messaging till about half past two last night. She's funny.'

*Yeah, she is*, Bradley thought as he forced a smile.

Chris caught up and nudged into him, almost knocking him over with the force of it. 'She seemed excited you were coming, man. I told her I thought Heather would be happy too. I think she might have a thing for you.'

Bradley blushed. 'Nah, she hasn't, but Avril seems to think that I like *her*. You guys aren't setting me up here, are you?'

Chris laughed and slapped Bradley on the back. The force was so hard that it pushed him forwards, almost knocking him over again. 'Not unless you guys are going to set me up with Sarik.'

Bradley's brow ruffled. 'Sarik? Sarik Patel? From the football team?'

Chris grinned and nodded.

'But you're not ...'

'Gay? Fuck, Bradley, what rock have you been hiding under? You need to get out more. I came out about a month ago. I'm loud and proud, baby.'

Bradley jerked back a little, putting distance between them.

Chris laughed again. 'For fuck's sake, man. It's not catching, you know. Besides, what makes you think I'd be into a fucking mess like you when there are the Sariks of this world?'

He was laughing loudly as his hands emphasised his words.

Bradley suddenly felt better about Chris and Avril's late night messaging sessions. He caught back up with the taller boy and, gripping the straps of his backpack, continued towards their destination.

The old Windsor place.

4.

AS THE MANSION loomed before them, Bradley could see someone shuffling around the chicken wire fence. *Too scared to go in?* he asked to himself.

It was Ted.

Ted was one of the happiest kids Bradley had ever known in his life.

'Chris, you big faggot, where did you dig up this weedy little vampire?' Ted shouted as they approached.

Bradley's face dropped at the use of the *F word*, but Chris was laughing and holding his arms out to embrace Ted. 'Come here, you fucking beach ball.' He laughed as his muscular arms wrapped around the wider boy.

'Bradders, Avril said you were coming; I didn't believe her, though. I told her you were too chicken.'

'Is there anyone Avril *hasn't* been messaging? Besides me, that is.'

Chris was laughing as he slapped Bradley's back again. 'Don't beat yourself up, Bradders. Ted's gay too.'

Bradley's eyebrows almost lifted off his head as he looked at Ted.

'Fuck off,' Ted shouted. 'You wish you could get your hands on some prime beef like this,' he shouted, grabbing his crotch.

Both Chris and Bradley frowned and looked away.

'Here they are,' Chris said, saving the assault on his eyes by turning his back to the two friends.

'Here come the girls,' Ted sang, clicking his fingers with faux sass as three girls approached them, giggling and pushing each other playfully.

Bradley watched Avril. She was dressed in just a t-shirt and jeans. He grinned as he looked at the other two walking with her. They were wearing jeans and jackets. *She's going to need my jacket after all*, he thought with glee.

'Hey, Bradley, your mommy let you out, then?' Samantha said as she beamed him a radiant smile that he knew was totally fake. Samantha was gorgeous, but she knew it, and she played to its strengths at every given opportunity. It was fair to say that he didn't like her much.

Heather was the quiet one. She was grinning too but never said anything to him or to the other two boys.

'Oh, Bradders,' Avril gushed. 'You've brought a spare jacket. You just might be my life saver tonight. If we survive Joe and Flo, that is.'

Bradley shook his head but was laughing. 'I asked my mom about Joe and Flo. She said they were a myth when she was a kid too.'

'Jesus, that long ago.' Samantha laughed, pretending it was a joke, but Bradley could hear the vitriol lying just beneath the surface. Samantha's mother and his mom had been in high school together, and there had always been a deep rooted dislike of each other. His mom said her mom was a bitchy little slut, and as he looked at her daughter, he could see the apple hadn't fallen too far from the tree.

She'd been dating Chris on and off for a while before he came out as gay, then she jumped on the opportunity and became his fag hag. She revelled in the prestige of having a gay best friend. *Especially one so hot,* was a direct quote. He'd have to keep an eye out for her tonight; if there was going to be any drama, it would come from her direction.

He flashed her his best sarcastic smile. 'She's the same age as your mom,' he countered. 'Well, the same age as most of her, anyway.'

Everyone got the reference.

'OK, you two, play nice,' Ted interjected, calming the situation. 'Are we just going to stand out here and talk about Sam's mom's false tits all night, or are we going in? Personally, I'm willing to do the tit talk.'

Chris didn't need to be asked twice. Even before Ted had finished his little speech, he was already striding up the stairs and pulling on the rotted wooden front door.

'If we're going in, we're going in,' Chris shouted as he strode confidently into the darkness.

Bradley watched him go. The moment he was inside, a shiver ran through him. He didn't know if he'd just had a premonition or if he'd seen this door before, but the situation was almost identical to the one in his dream. He was suddenly cold, which was odd, as the night was borderline warm. He had to stop himself from shouting, from protesting Chris going in on his own. He didn't want to look like a wuss, especially in front of Avril, and even more especially in front of Sam.

He felt an arm hook through his, and he turned. Avril was there, smiling at him. 'Come on, my knight in shining armour. If we're going to spend Halloween night in some fucking spooky mansion, then let's fucking go.'

Feeling boosted and braver than he had moments ago, he pulled her up the stairs and headed for the door.

'This is fucking stupid,' he heard Sam moan to Heather, who didn't reply.

~~~~

'Chris, where the hell are you?'
~~~~

The five of them entered the property roughly thirty seconds after him. Bradley and Ted had their flashlights on and were throwing beams around the expansive hallway. Everything was black and white in the stark illumination. The floor was strewn with leaves and rubble; there were ancient cabinets and bookcases leaning at odd angles against walls that were mouldy with fungi growing from them. The walls were peeling and crumbling, giving the room an odd look of an old and musty but rather grand tent.

The stink of mould permeated the air. It gave the house a cold, damp smell, not unlike a wet mop that had been left in a bucket for months or even years.

Bradley had a heart stopping moment when his flashlight beam happened upon an old painting hanging on the wall. The beam caught the old man's eyes, and for a split second, the stern figure jumped from the canvass and headed directly for him, his painted mouth hanging open and his fingers flexing into claws. When his heart started beating again and he realised it was nothing but an old portrait, he chuffed and looked at Avril, who, to his relief, hadn't noticed him jump.

This he was glad for.

He sighed and continued his investigations.

'Chris, come on, man. We know you're going to jump out at us. Stop being a slasher movie cliché,' Samantha shouted as she stood behind Ted, linking Heather.

Chris appeared from behind a large freestanding cabinet. He was fixing up his fly. 'Sup?' he asked as everyone looked at him. 'I was taking a leak. Is that OK?'

'Don't you think that's a bit crass? You know, you are in someone's house?' Bradley replied.

'Whose house? No one's lived in this dump for years, if you don't count Joe and Flo, that is.'

'Don't …' Heather said, surprising everyone, even Bradley, who had almost forgotten she was there. '…

mention them twins,' she finished. 'That story freaks me out. Can you imagine how their parents must have felt?'

'It's not true. It's an urban legend made up to keep kids like us out of this place,' Bradley explained. 'What I don't understand is why we've never been in here before. It's awesome.'

Heather shook her head. Her hands were buried deep in her pockets, and she refused to look anyone in the eye. 'No, there's something wrong here. I can feel it. It's just …'

'Ancient and abandoned,' Ted finished for her. 'It's supposed to feel like that, otherwise what's the point of a Halloween stay over? We might as well go and stay in a hotel somewhere.'

Bradley liked the idea of a hotel. Mostly because staying over with Avril would be exciting, but also because Heather's anxiety was rubbing off on him a little. There *was* something about this house; he could feel it too. It was foreboding and oppressive. It was niggling at him, telling him, in the words of a 1990's rock band his dad listened to, to get the funk out, to run away as far as he could before *everything* went to shit.

'I suggest we split up into teams,' Samantha said, eyeing Avril and Bradley as if they were something she had just stepped in. She did the same with Heather and Ted.

'What do you think this is, Sam? Scooby fucking Doo?' Ted replied, giving her a *are you really as stupid as you look* facc. 'We stick together. That way, we're all safe and no one gets lost or hurt. This building is gonna have a lot of rotting infrastructure. We don't want anyone falling and hurting themselves. Is everyone OK with that?'

Bradley looked at Ted with awe at his little burst of authority and maturity.

Sam closed her eyes and looked away.

'You won't be able to convert me anyway.' Chris laughed as he took her hand. 'You tried before, remember.'

Everyone else laughed except Sam, who rolled her eyes and removed her flashlight from a pocket in her jacket.

'OK, so before we start exploring, I need to know if any of you girls are on your period,' Ted announced. This elicited a groan of disgust from the three girls. 'I only need to know because I read somewhere that the menstrual cycle can attract ghosts and dark spirits. You know, like it does bears.'

Bradley was waiting for the laugh, for the joke in Ted's stupid question to reveal itself. When it wasn't forthcoming and his face remained serious, he realised that Ted was just Ted. He was neither authoritative nor mature.

'You are joking?' Avril asked, shaking her head when it became apparent, he wasn't.

'No. Seriously, I read it on a website. They said that the powerful emotions and the inner turmoil of a woman on her period can set off electromagnetic flares that attract spirits, poltergeists, and other supernatural entities.'

'Did they emphasis the *titties* part of that sentence?' Sam asked; apparently, she had gotten over her small huff about splitting up. 'Because I'm pretty sure whoever wrote that article has never even seen a woman—in real life, I mean.'

Ted's face creased.

'Come on, man,' Chris said, putting his arm around his friend. 'You have a lot to learn about women.'

'From a gay man?' Ted asked, his eyebrows raised.

Chris nodded, pulling him away from the girls, into the darkness of a nearby doorway.

The rest followed them across the dusty, rubble-strewn floor, to the door that led deeper inside the spooky house.

## 5.

THE HOUSE WAS bigger than any of them had realised. There were rooms coming off rooms, leading to corridors that had more rooms coming off them. They had been exploring for over an hour, and they still hadn't even touched a quarter of the downstairs. Never mind the upstairs.

It was a creepy old building. It moaned and groaned and complained as they entered every room; it whined at them creeping through its veins, grumbling at their very existence. Dust fell from the ceilings; things fell over that looked like they hadn't been disturbed since Nixon was President.

This was mostly due to Ted touching everything he could. 'I want to get a feeling for the house. To see what makes it tick,' he protested.

'I'm going to make *you* tick if you don't stop fucking with everything,' Sam snapped.

Ted grinned. 'Ooh, is that a promise? Are you going to try to turn me gay too? You know Chris has always wanted a slice of me, don't you?'

'Ted, shut the fuck up,' Chris warned.

Bradley could see Chris was getting sick of the joke. He was a big guy and always protective of Sam, even though no one thought she deserved it.

Ted backed off, walking towards the other side of the room, towards the remains of an old piano. He looked like he was taking an interest in it, but Bradley could see he was sulking. He continued touching the walls and shuffling his feet around the floor.

'Listen, I'm going to go upstairs and look around up there. This place is huge,' Chris said, looking at Sam. His eyes were urging her over towards him.

'No, don't go upstairs. Not on your own,' Heather cut in. 'You can't.'

'Jesus, Heather. Why are you always the voice of fucking doom and gloom?' Sam snapped.

Heather's head dropped. 'I just don't think we should be in here, that's all.'

'Well, we are, and I'm going upstairs with Chris. You guys can do what the hell you want down here.' She grabbed Chris's arm and pulled him towards the doorframe.

'Watch out for the twins,' Ted mumbled as they went.

'Fuck, I thought we were all going to stick together,' Avril offered, tightening her grip on Bradley's arm.

'Well, you know what thought did, don't you?' Ted asked as he walked away from the piano, towards the door frame.

'Where are you going?' Heather asked. 'We shouldn't split up.'

'Tell that to them,' Bradley snapped, instantly feeling sorry for the angry retort towards the scared girl.

'You can come with me, if you want,' Ted continued, holding his hand out to Heather.

She side-eyed Bradley and Avril as she made her way to accept the invitation.

'Go on,' Bradley said, his voice softer than it had been moments ago. 'We might as well get as much of this house investigated as we can. We're only here one night.' *Thank fuck*, he added in his head.

Heather looked at them as she and Ted left, leaving Bradley and Avril alone in the room, which was now much darker than it had been moments ago.

Avril turned on her flashlight and pointed it at him, momentarily blinding him with the intensity of the beam. He flashed his back at her, equally blinding her.

'Cut it out,' she laughed, lifting her hand up.

'You first,' he replied.

Her beam left his face, and for a few moments, he couldn't see a thing, as the light had imprinted itself on his eyes.

'Well, where're we going?' she asked. He liked the way she asked the question; it sounded suggestive and alluring but was probably innocent.

He shrugged. 'Do you think this shithole has a basement?'

Avril grinned. 'I don't know, but I like the sound of that.'

He felt his heart pound. He had wanted her to say no, to ask him to take her home, out of this place, and spend the rest of the night together somewhere warm, somewhere private. He sighed internally, then grinned. 'Come on then; let's go this way.'

~~~~

The house was indeed labyrinthian. Or at least it seemed that way due to the almost complete absence of light, the only exception being the narrow beams from their flashlights.

'I really don't want to be in here. I think we should leave.' Heather was lagging behind Ted, and as far as he was concerned, she was slowing him down, not to mention sucking all the fun out of Halloween.
~~~~

'Why don't you quit being such a moaning bitch?' he snapped. He hadn't meant to be mean, it really wasn't in his nature, but this girl was *fucking annoying* to the nth degree. 'Listen, if you want to go, then go. I'm staying, I like it here, but you're under no obligation to stay with me, none whatsoever.'

Heather was static. She'd stopped walking and was staring at him the way statues stare in museums. He flashed his beam at her. 'What are you doing?' he asked.

She was freaking him out now. *Why did I get stuck with the creepy weirdo? I could have had Avril, or even Sam, but no, Ted gets the weird chicks.*

'There's something in here with us, or someone,' she whispered.

He didn't want to hear this. He pointed his flashlight towards the strange noise he'd just heard behind him, where she was looking. His mind was already back in the land of Joe and Flo, the twins who never left this house.

There was no one there.

More importantly, there was *nothing* there.

'Do you want me to walk you to the door?' he asked, relieved.

She didn't move. He didn't even think she'd blinked, but then he couldn't see her eyes properly in the gloom.

'Come on, Heather, we can't stand here all night. Do you want to go or what?'

She moved her head, only slightly, and looked at him. 'It's too late,' she whispered. 'It's awake. We've woken it.'

'Woken what?' he asked, getting spooked by her theatrics.

She shook her head. It was, again, only a small movement, but it spoke volumes. Suddenly, he wanted out of this place. He wanted nothing more than to feel the night air caressing his face as he ran as fast as his body would allow, in the opposite direction of the old Windsor place.

He was starting to feel panic now.

It was in his chest. It was tight, like the air around him had become thin and difficult to breathe. He recognised it for what it was. A panic attack. That's all. He'd had them before and knew he could control them. There was no Joe, no Flo, there was no supernatural *thing* they'd awoken. It was just fucking Heather putting shitty thoughts into his messed-up head.

'Fuck you, Heather,' he gasped, trying to ignore the dizziness and the breathlessness. He turned away from her, heading off down the corridor in the direction the strange sound had come from.

He was hoping to bump into Bradley and Avril, or even Sam. They had to be more entertaining than *fucking* Heather.

~~~~

'Did you hear that?' Chris asked as he pointed his flashlight towards the stairs they'd just ascended.

'Don't, Chris,' Sam whined. 'It's not funny.'

'I'm not joking. I heard something over there.'

Both of them looked in the direction the flashlight beam was pointing. They were on the landing of the upper level, and if they wanted to, they could have looked down over the grand hallway.

Neither of them wanted to.

'Is there anyone up here?' Chris shouted, hoping no one would answer. He got his wish. 'I definitely heard someone moving around over there,' he whispered.

Sam held on to him tighter than she had ever done, even when they were together and making love, mostly because they both thought they should be rather than either of them actually wanting to—Chris because he already knew
~~~~

he was gay, and Sam because she didn't want him to ruin her hair.

They were compatible as friends, though, and regularly had each other's back. Right now, they were glad to be in each other's company.

'It was nothing,' Sam whispered.

Chris thought she didn't sound like she could convince herself, never mind him.

'Yeah, you're probably right. Come on, let's have a look in these rooms; maybe we'll find the remains of Flo and Joe.'

'Joe and Flo,' Sam corrected. 'And I hope we don't.'

Chris grinned. 'Come on.'

She didn't come. He pulled on her arm. 'Come on.'

She still didn't come.

He swung his flashlight around to face her. She looked right into the beam. He thought it must have been hurting her eyes, so he moved it. She didn't flinch at the beam's scrutiny. 'Sam?' he asked. 'What's up?'

She said nothing; she just pointed down the landing.

Chris swung his beam.

6.

'THIS PLACE JUST goes on and on,' Bradley whispered.

Avril was holding on to his arm for dear life, jumping at every little noise, at every little settlement of the house. He was enjoying the attention, even considered throwing something when she wasn't looking just so she'd hold on to him tighter.

'Do you think there really is a basement?' he asked, sounding braver than he felt.

'I don't know. Bet there is, though.'

'Should we keep looking for it?' He didn't want to go into a dark basement in an old, abandoned house. He was a fine connoisseur of horror movies, old and new, and he'd always criticized writers who sent their characters into such stupid situations. However, he wanted to look confident in front of Avril.

She sighed.

It was a reply, and not the one he wanted to hear.

They were at the foot of the stairs where Chris and Sam had ascended and disappeared into the darkness. He looked around and saw a small door next to the stairs. As he looked at it, he cocked his head to one side and exhaled slowly through his nose. He hadn't noticed it before and had definitely not noticed the fact it was open. He shone his flashlight through the small crack and saw stairs leading down.

His heart dropped into his stomach.

Avril looked at him.

He looked at Avril.

The question hung between them for a small while before it became heavy, too heavy to be ignored.

'Should we go down there?' he asked, cringing inside.

Her face said no. Her body language said no. Yet her mouth said, 'Yeah, come on. It'll be fun.'

Bradley hated her right then. He hated that he was totally in love with her and now had to prove himself by going down into a stupid, dark, haunted murder pit just for shits and giggles. 'We'll need to make sure the batteries are good in the flashlights. We don't want them cutting out while we're down there, do we?'

'Nope …' Avril replied a little too quickly.

She was rubbing her hands on her pants. Bradley thought it was a nervous reaction and grinned. *Let's get in, get out, and then get busy*, he laughed in his head.

He flicked his beam towards the door again.

For a moment, he thought he saw something lurking behind it. Something small and pale. His brain went straight to Joe or Flo. He jumped back, just a little, but the beam gave his cowardice away.

'Are you OK?' Avril asked; there was real concern in her voice.

'Y-yeah,' he stuttered. 'I just—'

'Just what?' she asked a little too quickly.

He shook his head, and a shaky, nervous laugh fell out of him. 'Nothing, it was nothing. Come on, let's see what's down there.' He moved forwards. There was real trepidation in his movements, and he thanked the darkness for hiding it from Avril. His hand reached for the door handle. As he watched it, pale in the beam of light, to him it was something out of a movie, something third party, something that wasn't quite his. He wanted to stop it, to not grab the little metal orb handle, but was unable to do so.

It just continued to grasp.

All sounds within the house ceased to exist, and all the smells. Even the presence of the ever gorgeous Avril next to him ceased to register. His whole world was this alien hand and the dirty, dusty door handle it was grasping.

As his fingers wrapped around the bauble, he didn't even register the cold or the roughness of it. He pulled it. *Don't*, he thought as if he were sitting on a sofa somewhere safe, watching these idiotic teens in their stupid movie doing stupid things.

Only the stupid teen was him, and it was his own movie he was starring in.

It was a reality flick.

'Is it stuck?' Avril whispered, snapping him out of his ugly reverie.

He looked up at his gorgeous friend. 'Huh?' he asked.

'Is it stuck? The door. Won't it open any further?'

His brow creased, and he pulled the handle again.

It still wouldn't move.

'Here, let me try it,' she said, pushing him aside and grasping the knob before he could stop her.

It swung open easily.

Perhaps too easily.

~~~~

There was something behind it, pushing it open, or at least that was what it felt like. Something that wanted her to step into the delights of the darkness and embrace whatever fate had in mind for her.

The stairs were steep. They were not the same grandiose stairs that ornamented the main hallway. These
~~~~

were steps of doom, leading down to the same dingy basement she'd seen in every single serial killer movie or documentary on that damned TV that she was missing right now. They were dark, concrete, and enclosed, making the stairwell feel like a throat, or a death tunnel, or something equally as creepy. Avril tried to swallow, but her throat was bloated and dry; it clicked as what little spit she had tried to slide down its own dark tunnel.

She pointed her flashlight into the darkness.

It was so thick that the beam failed to penetrate all the way to the bottom. All it managed was to cut through about half of the steps before petering off into nothing.

'Where do you think it goes?'

She looked at Bradley as if he'd asked the stupidest question she'd ever heard, mainly because it was one of the most stupid questions she'd ever heard.

He rolled his eyes as if acknowledging how stupid his question really was. 'You go first,' he urged. 'I'll, erm … take the rear guard.'

'We need to get something to put against the door. We don't want it closing on us and locking us down there. Not with Joe and Flo on the loose,' Avril teased. It was half a joke, but the other half of her was deadly serious.

'Good thinking.'

He walked off, leaving her alone, gazing into the entrance to the abyss.

The darkness was calling to her. Even to her addled, stressed brain, that sounded ridiculous, but it was. She could hear the siren song of danger, the seductive whisper of agonising terror.

'*Avril,*' it called to her and giggled.

She shivered as her light shone down the stairs.

The laugh came again, and she thought she could see something moving in the darkness below. Something shifting, undulating in the velvety blackness of nothing. She swooped the flashlight away from the mouth of madness and searched for Bradley. The unease she'd been feeling returned twofold. Her stomach was uneasy, and she felt like she needed to go to the toilet desperately.

'Bradley,' she hissed, wanting to both shout and conceal her whereabouts at the same time. 'Where the fuck are you?'

There was no answer.

A shout from somewhere in the house followed by another from a different location caused her to freeze. The flashlight slipped from her hands and rolled through the doorway and down the stairs. The lighting effect of the beam hitting each step, time and time again, was dizzying. She watched it fall, mesmerised by its journey … until it stopped.

There hadn't been that many steps she couldn't see initially, only about two or three more. Counting them to where the flashlight lay flickering in the darkness, she frowned.

*Why does there have to be thirteen?*

She looked behind her, hoping to see Bradley's light, or any of the others, ready to save her from having to go down those steps and retrieve the damned flashlight. Then maybe they could all get the fuck out of this madhouse without falling over anything and breaking ankles, legs, or, even worse, necks.

'Bradley,' she snapped again. She was angry at him for leaving her there. Thankfully, the anger was drowning out her fear. 'Where *are* you?'

There was another shout from somewhere in the house. This one sounded male, as opposed to the other two that sounded female. Even though the first two had freaked her out, this last one scared the bejesus out of her. Her heart was pumping in her throat; she could hear blood pumping through her ears as it rushed around her head, causing it to throb. She needed to get away; however, her flashlight was thirteen steps below, languishing on the basement floor. There was no way she'd be able to get safely out of the house without it. It was far too dark and far too treacherous. She swallowed, causing another dry click, and clenched her fists. Holding her breath, she stepped into the darkness.

It was like stepping into another world, or stepping into jelly, a black, ominous jelly. The air felt different. It clung to her, enveloping her. It was trying to suffocate her. Claustrophobia overpowered her, and she almost lost her footing. She tried to turn, to scramble back into the house, to escape whatever this was consuming her.

But she couldn't turn.

She was stuck, trapped on the stairwell.

She was forced down another step, closer to the still flickering flashlight on the floor. The light was distorted; it was as if she were looking through water. She was forced down another step, and then another, and another. The flashlight was almost within reach now. It was the only light source down there, yet she could feel the expanse of the open space around this odd prison.

It was cold, and the cold felt old somehow. That was an odd thought, as she knew temperature was timeless, yet this felt like it had been around for hundreds, thousands of years … *shit, maybe even a millennia.*

When she reached the bottom step, whatever it was surrounding her subsided, as if it had done its work bringing her down there into this everlasting, stark, cold darkness.

Free of whatever it was, she looked back up the stairs. There was just enough light up there to see the door.

Reaching down for the flickering flashlight, she did what every other person in this same stupid situation in all those ridiculous films did: she banged it against the heel of her hand.

The light stopped flickering and solidified. She breathed a sigh of relief before shining it up the steps towards the half open door. She was just about to climb up and start getting the *fuck* right out of Dodge, but the thought of whatever it was that had enveloped her on the steps sent another shiver through her. This one felt deeper and colder than the temperature that was currently clawing its way through her outfit. This cold was searching her flesh, hungering for any warmth it could feed upon, allowing it to grow. She could feel it eking into the temperate marrow of her bones.

*Bradley,* she thought. *He's up there on his own. What were those shouts? Are the others in trouble?*

She needed to get out of this dank, cold basement and help her friends. She needed to rescue Bradley and get everyone out of this shit hole safe and sound.

A noise from behind caused her to turn and whip the flashlight beam around to see what it could have been. Her heart was hammering in her chest, and she felt dizzy. She had no weapons to use against a serial killer, and if it was Flo and fucking Joe, she didn't think a weapon would be any good anyway.

There was nothing there.

There was *no one* there.

That was OK with her.

Only there was *something* there. Over against the far wall. She couldn't quite make out what it was, but whatever it was, it wasn't moving. This she was grateful for, but whatever it was, it had piqued her interest. She looked at the door at the top of the stairs and then back at whatever it was against the wall.

The cold was biting into her flesh, and she cursed herself for not bringing a jacket. The thought of the extra jacket Bradley had wrapped around his waist teased her. She needed to get out of this basement and back into the warmth of the night.

Whatever it was against the wall had other plans. It was calling to her.

'*Avril*,' it whispered.

It scared her.

No, it petrified her. Every last fibre in her body told her to run up the stairs, to get away, to get Bradley and get out of the house. They could then make out, have kids … live happily ever after. Her only emphasis was on the word *live*. Yet the stupid thing over the other side of the empty room screamed at her, demanding her attention.

Her feet started moving even before she'd instructed her brain to move them, and they were not going the way she wanted them to.

She wasn't covered in the strange air she'd experienced coming down the stairs, but she was experiencing the same lack of control. There was just no way of stopping herself from moving towards whatever it was caught in the narrow beam of the flashlight.

Right now, she wanted Bradley—or Chris, Ted, Sam, fuck, even Heather—to come down and save her, to rescue her from what was over the other side of the room, from what was calling to her. She closed her eyes and gave up the struggle, surrendering herself to whatever force was in control of her.

Then she opened them again, not wanting to trip over something and twist an ankle and not be able to run when she needed to—because she *knew* she was going to need to run at some point.

Any noises from behind her were inconsequential. Her whole physical focus was on the item, or items, as it was now obvious there was more than one. The force was controlling her body but not her mind.

'*All these kids are going to die,*' the voice she now knew wasn't just in her head screamed in a whisper. The words were coming from the two bundles propped against the walls. '*All these kids* have *to die,*' it continued.

'No,' Avril croaked as she drew closer.

The items were in focus now, two burlap sacks, the kind you might have gotten coal or potatoes delivered in. Only she didn't think they were filled with either of those commodities right now. There was something else making them bulge, something different packed inside the old, musty material.

They were frayed and decayed, covered in dust, years' worth, maybe more. There were holes where rats or other vermin had obviously chewed through, looking for food, trying to get to the tasty morsels inside.

Avril wanted to stop; she sobbed as she couldn't and kept on moving.

Eventually, she reached the sacks and could see what it was inside. One of them had something red sticking out of the top of it, the other had something yellow. Both colours were faded, almost not there, yet they popped in the narrow beam of light, the brightness looking almost alien in the gloom of the basement.

'*Avril, don't you see? All these kids are going to die. You understand, don't you?*'

'I don't,' she whispered. 'Why do they have to die?'

'*Open the sacks, Avril. Open them up and see why they have to die.*'

For the second time that night, she watched her hand do something she didn't want it to do. It reached for the first sack. She was willing it to stop, to return to her side, to do what it was told, but it was on a different mission, taking its commands from a different team leader, one that was in close competition to her own commanding voice.

She couldn't close her eyes either. She wanted to, as she didn't want to look into the sack, but it seemed that whatever was controlling her had different ideas. She was about to see, whether she wanted to or not.

Her hand, pale in the beam, reached the old cloth. Her fingers—*are they even mine?*—reached for it. The red thing inside shifted, as if it sensed there was someone close. As if it were alive, or at least sentient. She knew the whispering voice belonged to whatever was inside these bundles.

She knew it was true.

As her hand touched the cloth, it fell away from the red thing, crumbling as if it were million-year-old parchment decaying in the presence of fresh air. As it dissolved, the red thing revealed itself.

It was material; it looked like clothing.

Clothing that a child, or at least an early teen, might wear.

Her hand reached for the second bundle, and the cloth did the same thing, crumbling away, this time revealing a yellow top that looked about the same size as the red one.

That wasn't the only thing inside.

She had an inkling what it might be and had no desire to confirm her suspicions, yet once again, her hand had other ideas. She grabbed the faded yellow cloth and pulled it. It came away with the same ease as the sack had. Her eyes widened as they took in what it was inside.

She did the same with the red one.

It, too, came away with ease, revealing a skull beneath it.

Her body wanted to get away. She longed to put distance between them and her but couldn't. Her hand, the one not holding the flashlight, set upon another free-spirited mission, one to free the skeletal remains from both sacks.

The remains were small.

Not quite children's but not far off. She grabbed the red top and looked at the tag inside. There was a name written on it, faded and old, but in the flashlight, she could just about make it out.

Florence Addison.

She grasped the other one, the yellow one. There, in the same handwriting on the label, it read Joseph Addison.

*Joe and Flo*, she thought as control came back to her fingers and she let go of the garments. She fell back onto her rump. The flashlight slipped from her hands and rolled along the floor. When it stopped, she turned slowly, needing to see what it was that had stopped it.

When she saw, she realised she hadn't wanted to see at all.

There were two people standing behind her.

They were young. Maybe thirteen, fourteen at most, and about the same height. Even though both of them looked similar, the one in the red hooded top was feminine. They were both wearing jeans and sneakers. Avril's eyes flicked from them to the bundles. Other than the skeletons and the hooded tops, there were jeans and sneakers in both sacks that were similar, if not identical, to what the newcomers were wearing.

She wanted to scream but didn't have enough air in her lungs to facilitate it. Fear was suffocating her, smothering her. The dry air and the dust of years was stifling; the oppression of the death of children stole her very breath away.

They stared at her. Their eye sockets were nothing more than rotten worm filled holes in their pale faces, yet they burned with an unearthly light that shouldn't have existed. There was intelligence within that light, malevolence too.

As the children looked at her, all she could do was stare back.

She didn't want to breathe. She didn't want to smell these things. She didn't want them coming anywhere near her.

Her attempt to scramble backwards failed as if her feet were too heavy to move, as if someone had secretly filled her shoes with lead when she wasn't looking. They slipped on the dust and rubble of the cellar floor. No matter how hard she tried to lift her heavy limbs, they couldn't find purchase, and therefore, she didn't move any further away from the stoic tormentors.

As one, the ghastly figures raised their hands.

Fingers that were too long, too crooked, and too claw-like to be children's pointed at her. What little flesh that clung to the bony twigs was dark, dirty, and rotten.

Avril's scream came back then, with gusto.

## 7.

BRADLEY SAT UP.

He moved far too quickly for his head to compensate, and dizziness and disorientation engulfed him. He had to fight not to just flop back on the bed. His mouth was wide open, and he could feel a scream building up inside him, only it was reluctant to leave his body, as if it was too scared to leave.

He was cold.

He was also damp.

His wide eyes searched his immediate surroundings. They were looking for something familiar to rest on, to orientate himself as to where he might be. It was dark, too dark to recognise anything in the gloom. He felt around, his fingers stroking the soft furnishings he was surrounded with. He was sitting on something comfortable, something familiar.

The smell of a boy's bedroom filtered into his nose. And the same vanilla air freshener his mother insisted on plugging into his electric socket. 'Just to get rid of the smell of boys,' she insisted. He knew what smell she wanted to get rid of, so he didn't fight her on it. His shoulders relaxed, and he swallowed the scream that had been threatening. He rubbed his hand through his sodden hair and exhaled a long, shaky breath.

He eventually flopped back onto his pillow as his eyes adjusted to the dim light filtering between the cracks in the curtains, enlightening his recognition of his safest of places.

He was wearing pyjamas.

They, too, were damp and sticking to him. That was when the confusion of the situation kicked in. *What am I doing here?* It was a question that didn't sit right. The last thing he remembered was being in the old Windsor house, in the cellar with Avril. He had reluctantly followed her down after propping the door open but stopped at the bottom of the stairs and saw her looking at something over on the other side of the room. Something bundled against the wall.

There had been shouts. Loud, panicked shouts. They'd come from the others elsewhere in the house, but they hadn't had time to offer any help. Avril had opened the bundles, and then she'd begun to scream.

Her screams had been loud, perhaps too loud, and he remembered seeing something in the beam of his flashlight. He remembered seeing a shadow, only that didn't quite cover it. *Was it two shadows?* It was then Avril started screaming.

And he woke up here, in bed, covered in sweat.

He looked at the clock. It was almost three o'clock. He guessed by the dim light streaming in that it was three in the morning and not the afternoon.

*How the fuck did I get here?* 'This can't be happening,' he mumbled, swinging his legs out of the bed. His bare feet caressed the thick rug by the side of his bed. Flexing his toes, enjoying the feeling of the deep shag stroking his digits, confusion overwhelmed him. He leaned over and flicked on the bedside light. The sudden illumination stung his eyes for a moment before revealing the room to him.

Everything was as it should be.

There was no pile of clothing. He'd expected to see the clothes he'd been wearing in the house dumped on the floor with his flashlight next to them. Yet there was nothing. His room was tidy, undisturbed, as it usually was.

He picked up his cell phone and looked at the screen. There were a number of missed calls and quite a few messages too. He put his thumb over the sensor, and the phone unlocked.

Twenty-four missed calls, the majority from Avril, a couple from Sam, and some from Chris. The messages were from all of them.

How had he missed these calls?

He put the phone down on the bed and stared at the curtains. His thumb hovered over Avril's name. He wanted to call her, to find out what was going. He'd been in the house with them. He was sure of that. It was indisputable. He remembered thinking if he wore his extra jacket, Avril would want to stay close, for him to keep her warm, then the plan was for them both to …

He felt himself blush even though he was alone.

He looked at the clock again. No one would thank him for calling at this time in the morning. Not on a Saturday, anyway.

Suddenly, he was tired again. He turned his pillow upside down to the dry side and laid his head on it. Even in his confused state, his body obviously needed more sleep.

However, it seemed he had missed the sandman, and sleep was difficult to find. His brain was on overdrive, confused, addled. The sense of unease was too real. He could remember everything about being in the house. The stink of the must and the damp; Chris taking a leak behind a cabinet. He remembered Sam being a bitch and Heather being a scared little kitten, although both of those things happened on a daily basis anyway.

He remembered Chris and Sam splitting off, and then Ted and Heather.

He'd been happy to be left with Avril. He recalled being uneasy when they'd found the stairs to the basement. He didn't want to go down, but Avril did, and so they had. He had followed her down there, down the dark steps and into the blackness beyond.

He hadn't wanted to even step into the stairwell but also hadn't wanted to stay up there on his own, not in that fucking house.

There was a brief recollection of screaming from somewhere else in the house. He'd thought it might have been Heather or Sam. Both had a penchant for over dramatizing things, but when he really thought about it, it could easily have come from the basement.

His mind was fuzzy. He needed to call Avril to find out if she knew what was going on.

So, he did.

Avril answered on the third ring. Bradley relaxed as Avril's sleep fuddled voice mumbled a greeting. Even though her voice was thick, it was unmistakably her. 'Avril, are you OK?'

'Yeah, why wouldn't I be?'

'What happened last night? All I remember was—'

'What happened to you? You said you were going to meet us there. I really could have done with a spare jacket.'

He paused for a moment. *Is this a joke? Am I walking into something here?*

'I ...'

'You missed a great night. You really should have been there.'

*I was there*, he thought.

'Can we meet up?' he asked.

'Sure. Are you going to show this time?'

There was real humour in her voice, but he couldn't tell if he was being set up as the butt of an elaborate joke or if he was just going mental.

He hoped the former.

'I'll be there. Can we meet at the usual place, let's say about five o'clock?'

'Why not meet at the Windsor place? I'm still here. It's still Halloween, kind of.'

Something told him that wasn't a good idea, but he didn't want to sound chicken.

Reluctantly, he agreed.

When he hung up, he realised he was a lot more relaxed than he'd been since waking. He shrugged, trying not to think about the odd situation he'd found himself in. He lay back on his bed and sighed.

Then he got up, dressed quickly, and snuck quietly out of the house, grabbing a coat, as the early morning weather was a little chilly. He exited his street and headed in the direction of the Windsor place.

'I'm on my way,' he said to the voicemail when she didn't answer his call. 'I'll be there in about fifteen minutes. When you get this, give me a quick call. See you in a bit.'

He broke the connection and continued on the fifteen minute walk to the edge of town. He toyed with the idea of calling some of the others, just to see what they were doing, to see if any of them were still at the house or if they were having strange dreams, but he thought better of it. If he were walking into a prank, he wanted the circle of humiliation to be as small as it possibly could be.

The night was full as he strode through the small town. The streets he'd known all his life felt eerie. All the Halloween decorations were still out on buildings, fences, and people's yards. Vampires, ghosts, witches; that had all been kitsch to them earlier but was now giving him strange vibes. More than once, he imagined eyes following him from the decorations or a masked serial killer hiding behind hedges and fences, stalking him, waiting to strike. *I gotta stop watching those freaky slasher movies with Avril,* he laughed.

As he approached the house, he thought about how it had been there all their lives, yet no one had ever thought of staying over in it before. It had only ever been nothing more than a landmark to them, the town's spooky house. It only came into their peripheral over the last few weeks since Ted had the great idea for a Halloween adventure.

Yet there it was.

Looming over their town, where they'd hung out almost every day of their lives, through endless summers, spring breaks, falls, and Christmases.

Seeing it now, in the dead of night with heavy, grey clouds smothering it, emphasised just how spooky it was. It was sinister. Its dark windows were holes or eyes. Inside them, he imagined dark tunnels, gloomy staircases leading to basements where odd bundles were leaned up against far walls.

He shook his head, attempting to free himself of the images. It was odd to have vivid, almost total recall of a dream, as he'd never remembered his dreams before, not long after fully waking up. This one, however, was lingering. It didn't seem like anything could rid him of how vivid it was. He could swear he'd been there last night. 'Before a judge,' he added, shaking his head.

He looked at his phone. There was still no reply from Avril. He wondered if this had been a good idea. A kid alone in a deserted house. *What could possibly go wrong?* He took this time to collect his thoughts, to figure out what he was going to say to Avril. What he'd wanted to say to her last night, about taking their friendship one step further. He knew she felt the same, but they were having too much fun making each other squirm with their flirtations. That was always the most exciting part for him anyway. The wondering what it would be like when they *did* get together. Wondering if she would tremble in his embrace.

He was grinning when he saw movement in the darkness of the house's porch. *Maybe she's as excited as I am*, he thought. He stopped grinning then, thinking about what he was doing there. This was the craziest thing he'd ever done in his life.

'What did you want to see me about, Avril?'

He stopped in his tracks as the voice rang through the night. It sounded like Ted. He chuffed before continuing. He had an idea to hide in the bushes and jump out at them, scaring them all. He smiled as he imagined them screaming like girls.

'About last night. What the fuck happened in there?' That was Avril. It made him stop again. He turned his head, wanting to hear what they were talking about.

*Forewarned is forearmed*, his old man always liked to say.

'I don't fucking know. You just went all psycho on us, man. You're lucky Chris didn't kick your ass, girl or not.'

'It wasn't me. There was something in there last night. I'm telling you. I found these two bundles.'

'I know,' Ted replied. He sounded like he didn't really want to be there. This was strange, as Ted had always had a bit of a thing for Avril—well, her and every other girl in school, but they had always been close. 'You kept telling everyone. Why did you even bring that knife?'

Avril didn't answer right away.

*A knife? She's not the kind of person to carry a knife.*

'Protection.'

'Seriously? Jesus Christ, Avril. What did you think we were going to find in there?'

'Not what I did, that's for sure.'

This time, Ted didn't answer.

'We're going to have to tell the police,' Ted said after a too long silence.

'We're not telling anyone anything; you got that?'

'We can't keep this a secret. People are going to find out.'

'No one's going to find out. All we need to do is keep our mouths shut; it'll blow over.'

'It's not going to blow over, Avril. Things like this *don't* blow over.'

'What are you saying, Ted?'

'I'm not saying anything. I'm just freaked out by what happened.'

Bradley stepped away from the conversation. He didn't like where it was going. He pushed himself into a small copse of trees in the yard, a little away from his friends. As he did, he stepped on a twig, and it snapped loudly. He closed his eyes, cringing at the sound, but it seemed neither of them heard it.

'Do you not think I'm freaked out too?'

'You didn't look freaked out. You looked like you were fucking enjoying it.'

*Enjoying what?* Bradley shouted in his head. He wished he hadn't come to meet Avril now. He was scared of where this conversation was going. *Maybe it's all part of the prank they're playing on me. Avril knew I was coming to meet her, so maybe she's set all of this up as a part of the joke.*

He continued watching the heated exchange from just out of sight.

'I'm out of this, Avril. You can continue whatever sick fuck power trip you're on, but count me out of it.'

'Do you really mean that?'

'You bet I do. It's too much. I don't think I'll be sleeping much for the next week. I'm out'

Avril looked at him. Even through the darkness and the distance, Bradley could see her face was stoic, unreadable. Yet he bet her eyes told a different story. From the first time he'd met her, he'd fallen in love with her deep blue eyes. However, on the odd occasion she'd been angry or upset, they tended to turn dark, almost black. Like there were dark rings around them, like when Captain Kirk went evil and all they did to differentiate him from the normal captain was to give him some eyeliner.

Those were always their favourite episodes. Avril had called it guyliner, he had called it manscara, and they had both laughed. He remembered they had almost kissed on one of those nights, but his dad had turned up to take him home, as there was a heavy snowstorm heading their way.

*Good times*, he thought with a little sadness. This person talking to Ted seemed as far from his Avril as he thought it was possible to be. She looked and sounded like her, but …

'Fucks sake. Put it away, will you?'

When Ted shouted, it snapped him out of his little daydream of Captain Kirk, snapping him back into reality.

Instantly, he wished he hadn't.

He rubbed his eyes theatrically, knowing it wasn't going to make what he was seeing go away.

It was pretty much unbelievable.

Ted was backing away from her. His hands were raised, and although Bradley couldn't see his face, he knew he was serious. He was edging backwards towards the house, with Avril pointing a huge knife at him. Bradley had to do a double take to even recognise what it was. His breath was stolen again, as the girl he'd grown up with, fallen in love with, was now threatening one of their friends with the largest knife he'd ever seen. It looked like the one from that old movie with the guy who played the boxer in another movie. He'd momentarily forgotten the name, as it really didn't seem important in the grand scheme of things.

Ted was stepping backwards towards the darkness. 'Put it away, Avril. We're in enough trouble here without this.'

Bradley stepped out of the bushes, intending to follow them. He didn't want to go into the house, but he needed to stop whatever was going on before it got out of hand.

He needed to tell them that the joke had gone too far now. It had been all good and elaborate, but it just wasn't funny anymore.

He never got to do that.

He crossed the short distance from the copse to the wooden steps. He couldn't see them anymore, but he could hear them. They were still arguing.

Taking the steps by twos, he darted through the ominous doorway just in time to see Avril thrust the knife towards Ted.

Ted's hands went to his throat.

Avril thrusted again.

Dark blood began to pour from between Ted's fingers. It looked black in the darkness, and Bradley was still not sure if all this was fake. He couldn't see where the blood was coming from exactly, but he could see there was a lot of it.

Avril pulled the knife back.

It was dripping with the same darkness pouring from Ted's fingers. Her eyes were wide and excited; they looked lost in whatever she was looking at, maybe even drunk on it.

Bradley froze. He wasn't sure if this was real, but he did know that if it wasn't, it was a damned good set up.

It was then when Ted turned towards him. Ted's knees buckled, and he stumbled. His wide, scared eyes met his.

It was that exact moment when Bradley realised this wasn't a prank.

Ted's face was pouring with blood. Thick darkness was pouring from his mouth, and there was a horrible flap of skin folding over itself, hanging down his face. The knife had cut most of his nose off, and it, too, hung by a thread of pink flesh. His hands were at his neck, where the majority of the darkness was gushing between his fingers.

His knees finally gave up the fight to keep him upright, and he fell.

Stifling a scream, Bradley moved back behind the door, out of Avril's sight. He needed to get away from this madhouse, to run to the police to let them deal with this. Tears filled his eyes, and his breathing was rapid, too rapid. Too much oxygen was getting to his brain, and he could feel himself getting dizzy.

The house was spinning, the world was tilting, and everything was turning opposite. He recognised the faint coming and knew that the swoon would soon take him. It was the last thing he needed. If Avril could do something like that to one of their best friends, what would she do to him?

He dug his fingernails into the fleshy heel of his palm, hard enough to break the skin. He'd seen it done on TV shows and had always wondered if it worked.

It did.

The world swam back into focus. The smell of the early morning in late fall tickled his nostrils. Fallen leaves, pollen, freshly cut grass.

Now he needed to sneeze. He pinched his nose, and thankfully, the feeling passed.

A strange noise filled his ringing ears. It was a grunting sound mixed with something sickly wet, coming from where Avril had just kil—

No, he didn't want to think about what he'd just seen, not without the harsh reality of another panic attack rising. Although he knew he *had* to look. He needed to witness what was happening, especially now his potential girlfriend had turned into a fucking psychopathic murderer overnight.

He peered around the door, eyes half closed, not wanting to see what was happening.

There was something wrong, something apart from the obvious.

To Bradley, this whole thing was tilted. It was so far away from reality that there was absolutely no way it could be real. He and Avril had grown up together, grown close together. Yes, they enjoyed violent movies, serial killer documentaries on TV, they played violent video games, read the same books, loved the same pizza, but he would never in a million years think she could have been capable of … this!

It couldn't be real.

It was too far removed from reality.

Ted's twitching body was still bleeding out on the floor. He could hear Avril's deep breathing; it was fast, like she'd been running. A pool of darkness was spreading from beneath Ted's body; it was edging towards his hiding place. He could feel another scream rising in his chest, and the struggle to keep it down was real. The last thing he needed was Avril to know he was there, that he'd seen everything she'd done, and that he was a screamer too.

Hot vomit churned around his stomach.

He swallowed bitter saliva and cringed. There was no way he was going to be able to keep it in. He tiptoed backwards, out of the door, careful not to be seen or heard. Once the fresh air hit him, he ran for the trees.

Thick, bitter acid exploded from his mouth.

He bent almost double and continued to vomit, his hands gripping his knees as warm bile splashed them.

When it passed, he wiped his mouth and staggered off away from the nightmare, almost slipping in his own vomit. He headed away from the old house, from the bizarre murder scene and whatever else was happening there.

He scrambled to the fence that ran the length of the property and squeezed through the same hole he'd entered. Home was less than fifteen minutes away. He knew he should get there as quickly as possible, make sure all the doors were locked, and have a serious think about what to do next.

~~~~

Ten minutes into his journey, as he neared home, his cell phone rang. He looked at it, his heart pounding a heavy-metal beat from his desperate flight from the unnerving scene he had just witnessed and his inability to fathom what could have gotten into Avril. When he saw the name on the screen, the heavy-metal beat doubled, trebled, maybe even quadrupled. It was no longer just a rock song playing in his chest; this was thrash metal.

It was Avril.

He stopped and stared at the screen.

The picture was of her pulling a goofy face.

Now all he could see was her pulling that exact same expression as she stabbed Ted in the face with a huge knife while splashes of dark blood splattered over her.

Eventually, it stopped ringing.

It beeped, just once, and his heart almost missed a beat.

With a shaking hand, he pressed the button to connect to voicemail. 'You have one new message and … three … saved messages,' the electronic voice informed him.

He didn't want to, but he clicked on it anyway.

'Hey, sleepy, I hope you're up and ready to meet.'

*Did she just reference meat?* He thought about Ted lying dead on the floor of the old house, the pool of blood spreading underneath him. Bradley shivered.

'I've just been with Ted. He's such an asshole.' She laughed. The sound was chilling. 'I'll be at the house in about ten minutes. I just have to bury a chore. Call me when you get this.'

*Bury a chore? What the fuck did that mean?*
~~~~

It was a phrase they used to use when they were kids. Burying a chore was getting something done as quickly as possible in order to do something else, something a lot more enjoyable. However, at that moment, it had completely different overtones to it.

With his mouth dry and his eyes close to tears, he picked up the pace again, almost running the rest of the way home.

## 8.

BRADLEY THREW HIMSELF on the bed. The moment he hit the blankets his body began to shake uncontrollably. Tears that had been threatening eventually came with a gusto that surprised him. Once they started, he couldn't rein them in.

He couldn't remember the last time he'd cried but guessed it might have been over a stupid movie or something like that.

After a while, they slowed, and he was able to function again, at least physically. Mentally, he was not in a good place. His thoughts were everywhere all at once. He was in his horrible dream, he was in the house watching Avril do whatever it was she was doing with Ted, and he was at home, all at the same time.

With a heavy, shaky sigh, he looked at his window.

He tried to count how many times Avril had climbed up the trellis outside and gotten in through that window. The wind was making the curtains flap. Every time they did, he imagined her climbing in again, only this time, instead of having a video game controller or a DVD, she was covered in blood and grasping a knife.

A huge knife.

It was horrible.

He got out of the bed and closed, then locked the window. As he did, his phone rang again. It was Avril. He sat looking at the screen, at her goofy face that had seemed so funny at the time the picture was taken but was now sinister and murderous.

It stopped ringing and beeped again.

He selected the voicemail and opened it.

'Bradley, where are you?'

It was her, and she sounded normal, like she did every other day she'd been with him. 'I'm at the house. I've got something cool to show you. Hurry up. See you in a few.'

He continued to stare at his phone.

*Do I call the police?* It was a question that had been bouncing around his head since the moment he saw the knife. He wanted to, but what was he going to tell them? One of his friends, a high school kid, had gone mad and killed another of their friends at the old Windsor place?

*That's exactly what I should tell them.*

Holding the phone in his shaking hands, his fingers hovered over the number nine button, toying with the idea of pressing it and following it up with the one, twice. *This is Avril,* he reasoned. *It's a prank, all of it. It has to be. Just one huge prank. The whole town is in on it, everyone, including Mom.*

His rational brain told him that couldn't happen. Even though it was a small town, it was still too big to pull off a prank of this magnitude, not to mention how mean it was. However, mulling it over left only one reasonable explanation.

What did Spock, or was it Sherlock, always say?

*When you have eliminated the impossible, then whatever remains, however improbable, must be the truth.*

Avril was a murderer.

It was too much to consider. His exhausted, frazzled brain couldn't comprehend what was happening. He thought about calling Ted, just to see if he would answer or if it went straight to voicemail.

'Maybe Sam or Heather will know what's happening,' he told himself, his voice spooking him more than a little.

He almost dropped his phone when it started buzzing in his hands and then rang.

It was Avril again.

He didn't want to do it, but his fingers were acting on autopilot, and he swiped the green button.

'Hey, you,' Avril shouted cheerily down the line. 'Where are you? Are you gonna be a no-show again?'

'I'm … I'm …' *I'm what?* he asked himself. *What are you going to tell her why you aren't at the house meeting her?*

'I've got the shits,' he said in a panic, cursing his brain for coming up with that little snippet.

'Well, that's too much information. I didn't think we were going skinny dipping. We were just going to talk.'

'My stomach is killing me. I'm going to pass. Take a rain check till tomorrow. I'm just going to bed. I'm wiped.'

'Ted's dead'—

His stomach flipped with this information.

—'too. He said he was going to pass also. Hey, you two aren't …' She paused for dramatic effect. 'Doing a Chris on me, are you?'

'Fuck no, with Ted? If I was inclined that way, it would be with someone better looking than Ted. I barely want to be seen with you.' He laughed, although he couldn't feel the humour in the situation. All he could see was Avril's enormous knife plunging into Ted's ruined, bloody face.

His mouth watered, and he felt repulsed, pretty sick for real. 'I've gotta go. I think I'm gonna hurl. I'll call you later.' He hung up, dropped the phone on the bed, and ran to the bathroom. He barely got the lid of the toilet up before more hot bile erupted from his mouth.

He washed his face and flopped onto the bed again.

He closed his eyes and wished the day away.

9.

THE HOUSE WAS as gloomy as he remembered it. It smelt bad, like a week old rotting corpse. It reminded him of the time a raccoon had died in their school during summer break. No one had found it until they went back almost six weeks later. The stink had flooded the whole school, and they'd been given a vacation extension for it to be deep cleaned. The house smelt like that now, only worse. Bradley knew it was no raccoon causing the stink this time; it was the remains of his friend Ted.

He was wearing jeans and boots and a light jacket over a t-shirt and hoodie, layers to combat the cold.

With a flashlight gripped in his hand, he scanned the grounds, wondering what the *hell* he was doing there. The last thing he remembered was going to sleep in his own bedroom.

He had absolutely no recollection of coming back to the house.

He looked around the grounds, he checked his boots, he pinched himself to see if he was still dreaming. The grounds were empty, his boots were dirty, and he didn't wake up from the pinch. He could only assume this was real and he was, in reality, back at the old Windsor place.

Something must have called him back. He'd lain down on his bed with absolutely no intention of ever coming back here, but it seemed that life, or whatever surreal reality show this was now, had other ideas.

He was holding his breath as he entered the stinking building through the rotted front door and was instantly greeted with the grand staircase that Chris and Sam had disappeared up while Ted and Heather stayed downstairs. He remembered all of this as if it were only yesterday. *It was only yesterday*, he told himself. *If it even happened at all.*

His beam found the door to the cellar. It was slightly ajar. The darkness behind it was spilling into the gloom before it, like dark, shadowy fingers reaching, grasping for something just out of their reach. He wouldn't have thought it possible that darkness could infiltrate darkness like that, but he was watching it happen. It reminded him of an old toy he used to play with that was filled with water and oil. It used to fascinate him that the two liquids, no matter how much you shook it, just wouldn't meld with each other.

His heart was hammering. His eyes were heavy as if they needed to close, but there was no way he'd let them. He needed to know what was down these stairs and what had happened after Avril found the bundles.

Acting braver than he felt and ignoring the creeping darkness seeping from behind it, he gripped the handle. He'd expected it to be cold, but it wasn't. In fact, it was the opposite. It was warm, as if someone had been gripping it only recently.

He spun, shining the light around the grand foyer. The narrow beam illuminated corners, killing shadows that had been potential threats only moments ago.

Why had he come here alone after what he'd seen Avril do?

Satisfied there was no one creeping up on him, he returned his focus to the door. He swallowed, tasting the stink his nose had gotten used to. *The taste of the dead*, he thought before pushing the thought away almost as quickly as it had occurred.

He grasped the warm handle again and pulled. It opened freely, as if it had recently been oiled or recently used. He'd used it with Avril, going into the basement earlier tonight, or was it last night? *There are those fucking questions again*, he thought as his brain fizzed with the dichotomy it found itself in.

There was no way he could answer that question. His phone stated the date was the same as when they had gone into the house, October thirty-first, Halloween, but his body and his brain were telling him days had passed since.

He pointed the flashlight down the steps. The darkness was thick, oppressive, and almost total. The beam didn't make it to the bottom. He had to go down there, even though everything in his being told him not to. An ill wind caressed him. He didn't exactly know what an ill wind felt like, but if there ever was one, then the breeze that brushed over him from down there was one.

It brought the stink of the dead back afresh.

As it tickled his nostrils, it turned his stomach. He was glad his stomach was empty, otherwise the entire contents would have been all over the floor by now.

Something grabbed him.

It wasn't a someone, it was a *something*. His flashlight dimmed as he was pushed forward and enveloped by a something he could only describe as a cloud. This strangeness coerced him down the stairs. The pressure was slow enough for him not to be afraid of tripping and falling to his death down on the hard basement floor, yet it was forceful enough for him to be unable to resist.

When he arrived at the bottom, the cloud dissipated and warmer air rushed in. It brought the stink with it again. However, he was getting used to it again, as all it was now was a mere inconvenience rather than the all-encompassing, gut-wrenching reek it had been.

The beam illuminated the floor of the cellar. It was dirty, dusty, and covered with debris. On further investigation, he noticed footprints in the dirt. He figured they must have been his and Avril's from when she found the sacks. Taking a shallow breath, he flashed the beam around the floor, not sure why he was there or even what he was looking for.

What he found, he wasn't expecting.

It was blood.

It was fresh blood.

It was a trail of fresh blood.

Someone had been dragged down here and along the dirty floor. He hadn't noticed any blood on the stairs or in the hallway, but then he'd been acting almost on autopilot and had been guided down the steps. He turned and pointed the beam towards the stairs.

There was blood on every step.

Once again, he was hit with a wall of certainty that he didn't want to be there. He longed for his bed, for the safety of his home, for his mother and father. This house was taking too much from him. Cursing his stupidity, and whatever else it might have been that brought him here, he began to make his way up the stairs, careful not to step in any of the blood. He'd only gotten three steps up when the door slammed shut at the top.

It scared him, and he almost fell down the few stairs he'd climbed.

He attempted again, desperate to scramble to the top, to escape the oppression of this *fucking* basement, but his feet just wouldn't climb. They weren't stuck as such, he could lift them and move them, he just couldn't put them on the next step no matter how hard he tried. Panic was bubbling inside him as he realised, he could be trapped down there for a very long time.

*What if Avril's here?* he thought. *What about Joe and Flo?*

He turned to face the darkness all around him. The flashlight refused to cut through the gloom. *Just like last night.*

There was a small shaft of light over against the far wall. He scanned the dirty floor between him and it. There was blood.

Lots of blood.

He took another look up the steps. The door was closed, and he didn't want to attempt to climb them again. Something stronger than he was didn't want him to go that way. It was clear he had no other choice. So, uttering a small prayer under his breath, something he'd never done before, he followed the bloody tracks towards the shaft of light.

There was something leaning against the wall.

Two things, actually.

As he got closer, his light revealed what they were, although he already had a damned good idea.

They were sacks, brown cloth sacks.

They were the same ones Avril had found last night right before he woke up back in his bed, wondering how the hell he'd gotten there. He thought about the night, or the dream, or whatever it was, and wondered where the others could have gotten to, about who had been shouting, screaming, right before he did his little teleportation trick back home.

*'Bradley!'*

He turned.

His beam lit up the walls; it made him feel dizzy. 'Who's there?' he shouted. Only, it wasn't a shout; it was barely a whisper, and a croaked one at that.

*'Bradley!'* the voice hissed his name again.

The goosebumps up and down his flesh were nothing compared to the violent shaking of his body and the thumping in his head. His flashlight was shaking too. He had to hold it with both hands just to keep it steady. 'Who is it? Stop fucking around.'

He swung around to look at the two bundles again.

They'd moved.

They were now on their sides, their contents spilling over the dirty floor. It looked like old clothes, filthy with age and neglect. There were hoodies, one red, the other yellow.

'*Bradley!*'

'Fuck off,' he responded. 'Leave me the fuck alone. I don't want anything to do with—'

'*All those kids are going to die,*' the voice hissed.

He was trying to process what he'd just heard, but his mouth ran away with him. 'Who's going to die? Who are you?'

'*All of them ... One down, five to go.*' There was amusement in that voice, savage amusement. He didn't like it at all.

One of the bundles twitched; it was only slight, but it was there. He held his breath. He couldn't have explained it outright, but seeing the sack wriggle the way it did stole away his ability to breathe properly.

'*All of them will die, they have to ...*'

A shadow in the darkness descended over him. It reminded him of the darkness ebbing from the basement door earlier.

No, he'd been wrong. It wasn't a shadow.

It was two shadows.

His light focused back on the bundles.

They were now empty.

Bradley screamed.

<center>~~~~</center>

He screamed, and screamed, and screamed.

His bedroom door burst open, and he screamed again.

He pulled his blankets up over his face in the vain hope it would keep away the beast, or beasts, or whatever it was that had crawled out of those sacks. The ones that were now free to do whatever they'd threatened to do.

*'All those kids are going to die.'*

That was the threat. Ted had already been taken, and maybe he was going to be Avril's next victim.

Rough hands were on him in a moment. They were tugging at the sheets, and he fought to keep his only protection from being snatched away. His free hand felt around for something, anything that could be used as a weapon, something to fight Avril and her murderous cohorts' advances off. His fingers found the metal of the flashlight, and he wielded it as if it were a club.

As the sheets and blanket fell, he was ready to lash out, to smash his former love interest's brains out.

Only it wasn't Avril.

It was the shocked face of his father. 'Bradley. Bradley, you're dreaming. Wake up!' he shouted, covering his face from the oncoming attack.

'Dad?'

His father braved a peek over his arm. His face looked hopeful that he wasn't going to be brained with the flashlight.

'What are you doing here?'

'You were shouting in your sleep. That must have been some dream you were having; it was that loud.'

Bradley lowered the flashlight and looked over his father's shoulder at his mother, standing in the doorway. Her face was creased as she hugged her housecoat over her as if it were freezing.

'What's going on?' Bradley asked. His confusion was confounding his words, and he was finding it difficult to talk.

His father shrugged. 'Are you OK?'

He nodded.

'OK. Can you put that weapon down, and we can all get some sleep?'

Bradley looked at the raised flashlight and laughed, as did his mother, although hers sounded edgy, a little too high pitched.

They took turns kissing him on the top of his head before leaving the room.

His mother lingered a little longer. 'Why are you fully dressed?' she asked, almost as a matter of fact, as she left the room.

Bradley looked down at himself. He was wearing jeans and a hoodie underneath his jacket. He still had his boots on.

Exactly the same clothing he'd been wearing in his dream.

His boots were even dirty.

He dropped the flashlight on the bed and swung his legs down. There was mud, and dust, and—*is that blood?*—all over the sheets.

He inspected the stains.

It looked like blood.

He checked himself over; there were no cuts or scratches, so the only place he could think where the blood might have come from would be the basement of the house. He had absolutely no recollection of going back there. The last thing he remembered before entering the old Windsor place was lying on his bed, contemplating sleep.

He also had no recollection of getting back home.

He searched for his cell phone. He clicked it; there were fifteen missed calls from Avril.

There were no messages or texts. For that, he was grateful.

Sleep was over for him now. There was no way he'd be able to find that restful place again, not tonight. He looked at his phone again and logged on to the built-in location tracker app.

*Avril,* was his only thought. He clicked her avatar and the little ball spun. A map came up showing her at …

*The Windsor place! Where else would she be?*

He took a moment and selected Ted's avatar. It spun again before pinpointing him … in the same place.

He was shaking again.

*What's she doing with Ted's body?*

He looked on the social network app to see if anyone was active at this time of night.

Avril was.

As was Sam.

He clicked on Sam's location, and thankfully, it told him she was home. He debated whether to call her at this hour. Sam was a bit of a bitch, and he didn't know how she would react to a call at this time in the morning. He was just about to press the green button on his screen anyway, when the location tracker beeped, informing him she was moving. He watched as the app tracked her leaving her street, less than a mile from where he was now, heading towards …

'The fucking Windsor place,' he mumbled.

With his breathing becoming rapid, he pressed the green button anyway, regardless that it was almost three in the morning. He needed to warn her about Avril, about what she'd done to Ted.

There was no answer. 'Fuck,' he cursed, and began to type out a message telling her *not* to go to the house, *not* to meet Ted, and to return home and have nothing to do with Avril.

The message sent, but he got no read receipt from it.

He kept checking as he got ready to leave the house, which didn't take long considering he was already dressed for it.

He crept downstairs, hoping not to wake his family again, before silently slipping out the front door. Before he ran down the street, heading for the edge of town, following Sam's route, he stopped and looked at his phone again. He turned off his location for others to track him. He didn't want Avril knowing he was onto her; he also didn't want to go running into any kind of trap either. He set back off in a half run, hoping to catch Sam, but the faster he went, the faster Sam went too.

Even though he was panicking, running on adrenalin, it wasn't long before he was rewarded for his exertions with a stitch in his side, and he had no choice but to slow down and catch his breath. He took the opportunity to look at his phone, and a thought occurred. He realised he should also be tracking exactly where Avril was right now. He clicked on her name and closed his eyes. Another small prayer to someone, anyone, escaped him as he willed the tracker to tell him she was still at home.

She wasn't.

She was in the location of the Windsor place.

'Fuck,' he cursed breathlessly before getting himself moving again, faster this time.

Sam was almost there.

'*All these kids are going to die.*'

He didn't know if this voice was in his head, if it was a memory, or if the nasty hissing was talking to him, at him, somehow. He didn't want to linger to find out, so he set off at double pace, ignoring the pain in his side.

Whoever it was, or whatever it was, in his head was laughing, goading him.

He used it to spur himself on.

Eventually, inevitably, the abandoned house came into view. The sight of it chilled him to the bone. Ted had died there, at the hands of the girl he'd grown up with, grown to love.

He was still having trouble dealing with this reality.

The place looked deserted, but his tracker app told him a different story. Happy that he'd turned his locator off, he approached the grounds. Slipping through the hole in the fence, he went to the same copse of trees he'd hidden in before, the one where he'd witnessed the ugly side of his girlfriend and demise of poor Ted. Concealed by the branches, he peered out towards the old porch steps. He looked around to see if there was any trace of Ted's blood, but it was too dark to see anything.

Movement from the corner of his eye caught his attention.

His heart continued to pound—half due to his physical exertions in getting here so fast and the other in fear for his life—as he'd spied someone on the porch.

He stepped further back into the shadows of the trees and looked at his phone. Avril's location and Sam's were merged, meaning they were together somewhere close by. The app was accurate, giving the reader a vague but decent idea of where a person was or where they were heading. Right now, it was telling him they were close by, somewhere just ahead.

He guessed it was them on the porch.

Peering out of the bushes again, he could see more movement. In the darkness of the early morning, it was difficult to make out who it was, if it was Avril or Sam. He hoped it was neither. He hoped it was an old bum, or some other kids moving in on their turf, which he would gladly give up to them after what he'd witnessed earlier. However, he had the horrible reality of knowing exactly who it was.

An idea hatched.

Looking back at his phone, he called Avril.

He didn't hear her stupid *Buffy the Vampire Slayer* ringtone, the one she normally had set far too high, but the call still went through.

It wasn't answered. Bradley wondered if he'd done the right thing. It was late, or early, and if Avril looked at her phone, which he knew she had with her, as her GPS was turned on, then she'd know he knew something was wrong.

With his head starting to pound and his mouth drying up again, he peered out of the trees.

The two people on the porch were facing each other. He could see they were talking.

The shorter of the two, Avril, was raising her hands in the air as if explaining something to the other, obviously Sam. The other was listening. She kept turning away, looking behind her as if expecting someone else to turn up.

*Surely, they've seen my missed calls*, Bradley thought. *They have to be curious why I'm calling at this time.*

Then something happened, something that shocked him to his core.

Avril reached out an arm. She put it behind Sam's head and pulled her gently towards her. Sam went willingly.

They kissed.

Bradley didn't know how to take that.

On one hand, he felt betrayed.

On the other, he was aroused.

But mostly, after witnessing what had happened to Ted, what he'd seen her do to their friend, he was sickened. One part of him wanted to run up there and hit Sam for kissing his girlfriend, another part wanted to wait and see how far this strange but eroticised turn of events played out. Thirdly, he wanted to run up there and get Sam as far away from the psychopath that was Avril as he could.

*'All these kids are going to die,'* the voice hissed.

He could feel the pulse in his hands, in his neck, pounding. He could hear blood rushing through his ears. He was angry, hurt, scared. Every emotion he could think of was surging through him. It was fight or flight time. He needed to get up there and help his friend.

'*Is she even your friend?*'

This question, bouncing around his head, caused him to take stock of the situation.

'*She's a total bitch, and a self-absorbed one too,*' it continued.

'That doesn't matter. She's a person. She needs help,' he whispered, not believing he was answering the voice.

'*All these kids are going to die,*' it reiterated.

That made his mind up. He was determined to prove the voice wrong. Even if he might be losing his mind, hearing voices, and answering them, he'd witnessed Avril, his best friend in all the world, killing someone.

He needed to stop whatever was happening here.

Closing his eyes and pulling in two deep breaths, he strode out of the trees, towards the unaware lovers. He no longer cared about the betrayal or how sexy it was to watch these two kiss; that was over for him. He needed to confront Avril and get Sam away from her.

A thought occurred then.

What if they were in this together?

What if, when he stomped up there, all guns blazing, they both turned on him and he became Avril's next victim?

He was already out of the trees when this thought hit, and he stopped just short of making his presence known. He watched them for a moment, still kissing. There was no way he was going to lie to himself; his heart was a little broken right now. Avril had always been his. Everyone knew that. Yet here she was with another girl, one who was supposed to be, at least kind of, a friend.

Avril pulled Sam inside the house, and she went freely.

Bradley's heart broke again.

He didn't want to, but then again, it was also the only thing he wanted to do. He followed them inside. The steps creaked as he ascended them, but he didn't think the star-crossed lovers would even notice. They'd be too lost in each other's kisses to notice a jilted, jealous boy storming in after them.

They were halfway up the grand staircase when he got inside. He wanted to call out, to make his presence known, but something stopped him. It told him that was the last thing he wanted to do.

He crouched at the bottom of the stairs as they reached the top. Avril pulled Sam towards her again. She went willingly.

That was when he noticed something about their embrace.

Avril had her arms wrapped around Sam.

Sam in turn had her hands up, caressing her chest.

Only … she wasn't quite caressing her.

She looked like she was pushing her away.

Avril's arms were not hugging her, they were holding her, keeping her within her reach.

This was not the passionate embrace he took it to be; this was something else entirely. There was violence in it; there was struggle. There was also blood.

Most of it was pouring from Sam's face, from her chin and her mouth, where Avril was … biting her.

Her mouth was working extra hard on Sam's face, and Bradley could see chunks of something glistening on the floor where they were standing.

Sam managed to pull away from Avril, just for a moment, and something wet fell from her mouth. It was thick, and it hit the floor with a horrible splat. It took Bradley a moment to realise he'd just witnessed something nasty.

Sam staggered back from her attacker.

Even in the darkness, Bradley could see Sam's face was ruined. Her lips had been chewed. What was left of them were swollen and dripping blood. But the worst part was the thick darkness oozing from the hole that had once been her mouth, the space where her tongue used to be.

Bradley mimicked her movement and fell back too.

Sam's legs began to buckle, and she struggled to stay upright. She grabbed hold of the banister and was in some danger of falling over, plummeting to her death on the hard floor below. Avril grinned a bloody grin and reached for her, saving her from the fall. As she did, she tore her top open, exposing a bloodied sports bra beneath. Bradley guessed it had once been a pastel colour, but now it was dark and covered in what could only be described as gore.

With her other hand, Avril produced the same knife she'd used on Ted.

Bradley was struggling to breathe. He couldn't believe he was about to witness this again. Without any preamble, Avril thrust the knife into Sam's chest. It went in hilt-deep, almost without resistance. The girl's eyes opened wide on her destroyed features. They locked on Avril. There was shock, horror, and sadness within them. Bradley didn't know if he was just pouring his own emotions into what he was seeing, as it was too dark to really tell, but he knew that he'd already seen too much.

Or had he?

He couldn't leave.

Was there something stopping him from going, or was there something he was supposed to see? He couldn't answer either of those questions but did know that for some reason, he was frozen to the spot.

'*All these kids are going to die,*' the disembodied voice whispered again.

That was when he realised that *he* was one of these kids.

Sam fell then—or dropped would have been a better description—onto the landing. Avril stood over her, laughing.

Sam, with the knife still protruding from her chest, was on her knees before her attacker.

Avril took hold of her long, blonde hair and pulled her head back. Bradley gasped as Avril laughed again. She pulled the knife from Sam's chest; it came away with a little more difficulty than it had gone in with. She held up the large, dripping weapon and regarded it.

Bradley's eyes were drawn to it too.

It was just too unreal to think she owned such a thing.

This whole scenario was unreal.

'This might sting a little.' Avril chuckled as she pressed the dripping blade to Sam's stretched neck.

Sam murmured something; Bradley couldn't understand what it was, not from that distance, plus the fact that the poor girl had no lips to form the words.

Bradley was grateful that Sam was too far gone to realise what was about to happen to her. He turned away, not wanting to see.

The sounds were hideous.

Sam's attempts to scream were muffled as the knife sliced through her. The sinews, tissues, and bones of her neck offered the sharp blade surprisingly little resistance.

Bradley staggered back even further. He scrambled away, distancing himself from what he was seeing. This felt worse than what had happened to Ted. *It's not worse*, he scolded himself. *It's equally as bad. That's exactly what it fucking is.*

Crawling backwards like a crab, he made it to the door, then corrected himself and hid behind it. He wanted to hurl again, to vomit up the hot bile that was currently sloshing around his stomach. His stomach must have been empty, as even though he retched, nothing was expelled except a little spit.

He could still hear the noises coming from the landing; they were echoing around the empty house. Whether they were actual noises or ones his nightmarish imagination was conjuring, he didn't know, he didn't care either. It was enough just to hear them.

His phone was in his hand.

His hands were wet, shaking, and freezing. He struggled to even hold the device as his stubborn fingers kept missing the buttons he wanted to push.

He tried for the nine, then the one, and the one again.

Eventually, he hit the right combination, and the line rang out.

# 10.

HE WAS BACK in bed.

His eyes looked up at the dark yet familiar ceiling he'd looked at all his life. His heart was thrashing, and he felt warm, a little too warm. As he moved, jumping up in surprise and shock, he wondered what had just happened and how he'd gotten back here. 'What the fuck?' he mumbled through sleep infused lips. He looked down at himself, hoping beyond hope he would be dressed in his nightwear, shorts and a baggy t-shirt.

He wasn't.

He was dressed exactly the same way he'd woken up last time.

He looked at the clock. It still wasn't three a.m. *Seriously? What the fuck is happening?* He shivered when he thought of the dream he'd just had. It was horrendous. He reached for his phone. There were six missed calls from Avril.

The sense of dread he felt when he saw her name on his phone was palpable. It made him ache. He wanted to cry for Ted and for Sam but couldn't. Tears wouldn't flow. All he wanted to do was drop the device, let it smash on the floor, then scream himself to sleep. He wanted nothing to do with Avril, not after what ...

*What?* he asked himself. *After what? What's she done?* If everything was just a dream, then why shouldn't he call her back? *It's my brain fucking with me. Is it because of the feelings I've got for her? Am I trying to sabotage my own feelings?*

He looked on social media.

Avril had been online twenty-seven minutes ago.

Ted and Sam were showing as offline.

Chris was online; Heather wasn't.

Heather very seldom was.

He thought about messaging Chris. Reaching out to him, just to feel some kind of connection. His finger was hovering over the message app when he changed his mind and turned on the GPS tracking app instead.

He selected Avril first, then Sam. Neither were broadcasting.

Chris was. He was at home, by the looks of it.

Ted wasn't broadcasting, but Heather was.

Bradley's heart dropped into his stomach as if he were on the worst, most dangerous rollercoaster in the world.

Heather was moving.

Bradley didn't need to know where she was heading. He could guess.

'Fuck this,' he said, and called Chris.

'Hey, you,' Chris answered almost immediately, sounding cheery.

*He must have been talking to Sarik*, he thought. 'Chris, are you at home?'

'Yeah, I've just been—'

'Listen. Heather is out.'

'She's out? Like she's gay or something?'

Bradley shook his head. 'No, fuck no. Why is everything about being gay with you? She's out of her house. I'm tracking her on the GPS.'

'Weird much?' Chris laughed. 'Are *you* coming out? It sounds like you're protesting too much.'

'Chris, I think she's in danger. Have you spoken to Avril?'

'Avril? Nope. Not since the—'

'If she calls, don't talk to her. Don't meet with her. She's done some …' He paused, wondering how he should put this. 'Bad things,' was all he could think of.

'If you two have been fighting, I'm not taking sides.'

'We're not fighting, Chris. She's killing people. She's already killed Ted and Sam. They're both dead, Chris. In horrible ways. Both at the house, the old Windsor place.'

'The house? Bradley, are you high?'

'Will you please listen? Avril killed Ted and Sam.'

'Bradders, I was just talking to Sam about twenty minutes ago. She was very much alive. Believe me.'

Bradley was shocked into silence at this revelation. *How long ago was my dream? Was it a dream? Is Avril really killing people?*

'Will you meet me?'

'Meet you? Now? I'm in my fucking PJs.'

He started to sob. 'Please, man. Either Avril's a killer or I'm losing my mind. Heather is out of her house, and I'm tracking her signal now; she's heading towards the house.'

'Maybe she's met someone. Did you think about that before accusing one of our friends of being a female version of Ted fucking Bundy?'

'Please, Chris.' He was full crying now. Tears mixed with mucus were running into his mouth. He had to wipe the saltiness away before he could talk.

There was a long sigh over the other end of the phone. 'Fuck's sake, Bradders, no need to get all dramatic about it. OK. I'll be outside your house in twenty minutes.'

'Can you make it sooner? Heather could be in real trouble.'

He listened as Chris breathed on the other end. 'Five. Be outside.'

'Thank you. Seriously. Thank you!'

11.

'WHAT'S ALL THIS about Avril being a murderer?' Chris asked as he stood at the end of Bradley's path.

It was Bradley's turn to sigh. He shook his head, battling away his tears. 'I don't know. I don't know what's real and what's not anymore.'

Chris pulled him close and hugged him, his strong arms giving him reassurance. It was what he needed.

'Heather,' Bradley sobbed. 'She's at the house.'

'The Windsor place?'

'Yeah,' he replied, moving away from his friend, and wiping away his tears. 'We've gotta go.'

'Come on. I can't see Avril, of all people, being a serial killer. A serial pain in the ass, maybe.'

Bradley tried to laugh. 'I hope she's not,' he replied, straightening his jacket from his friend's crushing hug. 'But I have to know. Thanks for this, man. You don't know what this means to me.'

'You're gonna owe me when you find out this is a load of bullshit.'

He nodded as they walked off, heading towards the old Windsor place. 'Gladly!'

~~~~
~~~~

'Please, Chris. Please tell me that we all went into the house the other night,' Bradley pleaded as they walked. He knew how crazy the question sounded, but he no longer cared. Watching two of your friends die at the hands of someone you cared about could do that to you. He'd been dying to ask the question ever since they'd hugged outside his house.

Chris looked at him, his head cocked.

'Please don't mess with me, man. I know how fucked up it sounds, believe me. Just tell me that we all went in.'

His brow creased. 'Bradley. *We* went in,' he said.

It was like a weight, lifting off his shoulders. Suddenly, he felt lighter, freer than he'd felt over the last … well, he didn't know how long it had been. 'Thank God for that.' he sighed. 'I've honestly been thinking I'm nuts. Because I remember us all splitting—'

'Bradley,' Chris interrupted.

He stopped talking and looked at his friend. His eyes did not hold any relief for him.

'When I say we went in, I mean me, Ted, Avril, Heather, and Sam. You didn't turn up.'

'Don't fuck with me now.'

Chris was shaking his head. 'Bradley, I'm not fucking with you. It's three in the morning. I'm not in the mood for jokes. Avril told everyone you'd chickened out. Well, actually, she said you weren't feeling well.'

'That's a fucking lie,' he snapped. 'It was me who talked her into going in. She didn't want to do it. Jesus, her mom will back me up on that one.'

'I don't know what you want me to say, Bradders. You weren't there. Honest, I'm not lying to make this into some kind of stupid prank. We met up outside the fence. Avril came late. We didn't split up either. We all stayed together, and nothing really happened.'

'Did you go down into the basement?'

Chris's eyes looked pained as he shook his head. 'There is no basement, man. The house is built on solid rock.'

'No, there's a fucking basement. I've been down there twice now. The door is right next to the stairs. That's where Avril found the bundles; it's where she dragged …' He stopped. He could hear the desperation in his own voice, and it sounded pathetic. 'Chris. Honest. I've been down there. I was with you guys. I was. Fuck, you were talking about Sarik, about how you were into him.'

Chris laughed. 'That's hardly news.'

'I know, but it's what we were talking about. There was some tension. Nothing major, but you and Sam went upstairs. Ted and Heather wandered off, and me and Avril found the door to the basement. She went down first and found some bundles. When she unwrapped them …'

'Go on,' Chris said when he paused.

'Then I woke up at home, in bed. What the fuck is happening with me? Am I going crazy?'

Chris shook his head and pulled him close again. He wrapped his big arms around him. Bradley allowed it.

'Can we just get moving?' Bradley asked, a little embarrassed from the hug. 'I don't like the idea of Heather at the house on her own, or with Avril, for that matter.'

'Come on,' Chris said, pulling Bradley along at a faster pace than he was used to.

~~~~

They reached the outskirts of town in record time. The house loomed over them, watching them arrive, welcoming them like a spider welcomes a fly. Bradley looked at his phone. Heather's signal was still strong, informing him she was here somewhere.

'Heather,' Chris shouted.
~~~~

'Shush,' Bradley hissed. 'Don't let her know we're here.'

'Let who know?'

'Avril. She might kill Heather just to get away from us.'

'Avril,' Chris shouted next.

'Fuck you, man,' Bradley snapped. 'I'm not joking here. I watched her kill Ted and Sam.'

Chris was laughing as he shook his head.

'If you're going to be an asshole about it …' Bradley snapped before storming off.

'Bradley, come on; I was just fucking around.'

He ignored him and walked off in the direction of the hole in the fence. He slowed as he got there. Looking through, he scanned for someone, anyone who might be lurking in the grounds beyond. He couldn't see anyone, but he knew that didn't mean there wasn't any danger. The shadows were deep, and they hadn't thought to bring their flashlights this time. There hadn't been enough time.

He strained to look into the shadows. There was a silhouette by the porch that looked like it might have been a person, but it seemed too still.

He clambered through the hole and skulked through the overgrown gardens, his boots getting wet from the early morning dew on the grass. The silhouette turned out to be a tree, harmless and still. He turned to see Chris struggling through the fence. This calmed him and offered him a much needed courage boost, enough to enter the house.

As he approached the gloom, a noise caught his attention.

It was a shout, or it might have been a scream.

He stopped as Chris rushed past. 'That was Heather,' he panted.

Bradley watched Chris take the porch steps two by two and dart straight into the house. There was no hesitation, no looking back. He ran inside and was consumed by the darkness.

'Chris! Don't!' Bradley shouted, throwing caution to the wind of Avril realising they were here.

When Chris took no notice of him, he sighed and followed the bigger youth inside.

Once again, it was déjà vu. He'd been inside this house at least three times tonight. Whether that was physically or in his dreams, he couldn't tell. However, the ominous dread was the same, the cold darkness was the same, and the stink was the same too.

Abattoir chic!

'Chris,' he shouted again as he saw him running up the grand staircase. There was another shout, a scream. It was definitely female and was coming from somewhere on the upper floor.

He followed Chris. He didn't want to but did anyway.

By the time he got up there, Chris was gone. He looked both ways, up and down the corridor, but there was no sign of him. *Fuck, Chris. Where are you?*

A third shout sent shivers up and down his spine and set off a queasy feeling in his stomach. His mouth was already dry as he looked towards the room where the third shout had come from.

He was relieved when he saw Chris in the doorway.

'Chris,' he whispered, getting his attention. 'I think there's someone in there,' he continued, pointing behind him.

Chris didn't move.

'It might be Heather. If she's in there, then Avril must be somewhere close. You didn't see anyone, did you?'

Still Chris didn't answer.

'Chris?' he pressed.

Then the large youth fell on him.

The gaping hole in his neck spewed thick warmth all over him.

Chris's eyes were wild. They couldn't focus and were lolling around in their sockets.

As Bradley screamed, warm, salty blood poured into his mouth, stifling it. He gagged as some slipped down his throat, into his already fragile stomach.

Chris was heavy, far too heavy for him to support, and the sudden weight forced Bradley over. He hit the floor, banging his head.

'*All these kids are going to die,*' the voice in his head hissed as the world swam around him. His vision doubled, then trebled before returning to some semblance of normality.

Chris was crushing him and was bleeding out all over him. The gurgling from his open, bubbling mouth was making him sick, along with the taste of the boy's blood in his mouth.

He wanted to scream again, and again, and again, but didn't dare. He couldn't take the chance of swallowing any more of Chris's blood or giving away his location to Avril.

A shadow loomed over them as he struggled underneath the bigger boy. He looked over Chris' shuddering shoulder and saw what was causing it.

Avril.

Bradley stopped struggling. He didn't think she'd noticed him underneath Chris, who was currently dying on top of him. Chris was weakening; Bradley could feel life ebbing from him as his thrashings and shuddering slowed.

Avril's eyes were glazed. It didn't look like there was anything behind them. No malice, no evil intent, no thought, no conscience. All her attention was on the dripping knife in her hand, as if Chris dying before her was inconsequential. Bradley took advantage of this and slid from underneath Chris, using the slickness of the spilled blood to manoeuvre himself out. He hated letting go of his friend, but he needed to get away from the thing that looked like Avril.

It had Avril's beautiful face, it had her hair, but there was no way it had her soul or personality because murder and mutilation, they were not the girl he knew.

He rolled away from the almost dead body of Chris and into the shadows of the corner of the room. He held his breath as a now salivating, maniacal Avril fell upon the twitching body of Chris. The knife, which looked to have gotten somewhat bigger, was thrust into Chris's back.

Bradley closed his eyes; he couldn't watch. There was no way he could bring himself to witness the violation of the remains of his good friend by another good friend.

But though he closed his eyes, he couldn't close his ears. The sounds—the ugly laughing, the wet tearing, and the suction as she repeatedly thrust and pulled the knife— were disgusting. All he could think was he was glad Chris was already dead and therefore didn't have to endure this violation in life.

'*All these kids are going to die, Bradley,*' the hissing voice whispered in his head.

He didn't want to open his eyes; he didn't want to see what the thing Avril had become was doing to Chris. It was too surreal, too unimaginable to even contemplate.

'*They're all going to die, Bradley,*' the voice hissed again. It reminded him of the noise of water draining out of a bath. It was wet, unnatural, vile.

*They're dead already, or most of them, anyway. So, what do you want?* He wanted to scream that, to shout defiantly at the voice of whatever it was, or whatever had possessed Avril, whatever had slithered into her in this house, turning her into a psychotic killer.

'*You know what we want,*' the voice replied.

It then broke into laughter like it had heard the funniest joke in years. The sound hurt Bradley's ears, almost to the point where he felt they might be bleeding.

The laugh continued its rhythmic, high pitched, and repetitive cackle.

~~~~

His phone was ringing.

It woke him.

He took a quick gasp of air. It was warm and muffled. It took him a moment to realise he wasn't cowering in the corner of an old, deserted house but was in a bed. His bed. Tucked under the covers, listening to his phone ringing.

He snapped awake instantly, flinging the covers from him and reaching out for the phone on the table next to the bed.

He was fully dressed, but he'd expected that after the last few times.

He grabbed the vibrating device and looked at it.

Avril.

It was the same goofy photograph, the sinister one now that she was no longer the girl he'd known back then.

His heart was pounding again.

He didn't want to answer it, not her. However, he had to do something, as the ringtone was loud and likely to wake his parents. He meant to turn it off, to refuse the call, but in his hurry and panic, he swiped the green button instead of the red one.

'Bradley? Bradley, are you there?'

It was Avril's voice. It wasn't the ugly hissing voice he'd been expecting. She sounded tired, cold, scared. Her voice was rushed, and she was whispering as if trying to be heard down the phone but nowhere else.
~~~~

'Bradley. Help me. I'm trapped. I'm stuck here. Heather …'

Bradley put the phone to his mouth, ready to talk, to let her know he was there.

## 12.

WHAT ABOUT HEATHER? It was the only thing on his mind as he got ready to leave the house on this, the night of all nights. It was now the fourth time he'd left to go to the old Windsor place. This time, he was determined to find out what was going on with Avril. To see if she was in some kind of trouble or if she really was just into killing their friends. Or even if their friends were dead at all. He was going to sort this mess out, once and for all.

He looked at his phone. It was almost three in the morning, and none of his friends were online. He didn't care, he sent a message out to all of them anyway.

I NEED 2 KNOW IF UR ALL OK.
PLSE RESPOND ASAP

He didn't expect any responses, not at this time in the morning, and especially not after seeing they were all offline, but it didn't stop him wanting, needing them. He called Avril. When the call failed, he tried Heather, but there was no answer. He seethed, wanting to throw the damned device against the wall.

He went outside to the garage and rummaged around, looking for something, anything he could use as a weapon for if and when Avril came for him. He came out sporting a pretty heavy hammer. It wasn't quite the chainsaw he'd wanted, but it was probably a lot more practical. He couldn't be seen walking the streets of his town holding a chainsaw at three in the morning, heading towards a deserted house where most of his friends had already been killed, could he?

He checked his phone for any replies; there were none. So he checked the social network to see if anyone had come back online; no one had. He checked the GPS and was surprised to find Heather out and about. What he wasn't surprised about was the fact that she was in the vicinity of the old Windsor place.

'Avril, and whatever is in your head, I'm fucking coming for you,' he said aloud, marvelling at his breath leaving his mouth in a pluming mist.

## 13.

THE OLD HOUSE was just as he knew it would be. *Why would it be any different? It's the same damn night.*

He gripped the shaft of the heavy hammer in his hands and approached the hole in the fence, where all of this nightmare had begun. He was determined to not let Heather die this time, to not let her down like he had all the others.

As he got close, he checked Heather's signal. It was close. He knew she'd be somewhere around the porch steps. Maybe Avril had already gotten her and was in there right now, dragging that knife across her throat.

*Where did she get that thing?* he pondered, making his way slowly towards the door.

A silhouette caught his eye in the overgrown grass.

He could hear talking, whispering, like someone arguing. He recognised one of the voices immediately. They had whispered to each other like this on many, many occasions.

It was Avril.

He looked in the direction it was coming from and saw them. Avril and Heather, standing by the small copse of trees where he had hidden earlier, when the same fucking scenario played out but with Ted instead of Heather.

'No, Avril. I'm not going back in there,' Heather protested; she wasn't whispering now.'

'Heather, you have to,' Avril replied.

'You can't make me,' she said, turning away from her.

'That's where you're wrong.'

This reply was cold. It chilled Bradley, and suddenly, he wanted to shout, to warn Heather away from his psycho nearly-girlfriend.

Heather began walking away from Avril. *Go on, girl,* Bradley willed her. *Get to the fence. Get the fuck out of here.*

She didn't make it.

Bradley had an inkling she wouldn't.

Avril pulled out the knife. Even from this far away, it looked huge. She didn't hesitate in sticking the lethal thing deep into the middle of Heather's back. The girl buckled instantly. Her legs gave way, and she fell backwards, right into Avril's waiting arms. She dragged Heather's lifeless body through the grounds, heading towards the porch steps.

Something inside Bradley screamed again. He had to follow them inside.

'Why me?' he asked the chilly night.

The grass was disturbed, and the trail was easy to follow, even for someone not as used to following clues as he was. He cursed himself for not being brave or strong enough in character to shout out, to startle Avril, and maybe, just maybe, save Heather's life.

But he hadn't been.

When the moment of truth came, he chose the well-worn way of the chicken. *Keep your mouth shut, or you might be next.* He couldn't understand why he hadn't been chosen; he'd witnessed all the murders, every one of them. His own eyes had seen it happen in real time, in glorious technicolour. He hadn't understood how to process this information. His brain and body were confused; he didn't know when he'd last had any sleep, any real sleep, because every time he dropped off, everything came back to this place, the old Windsor place, and to his friends.

How could all of this happen? How could one person go from being a normal, everyday girl, his best friend, and the girl he wanted to become his girlfriend to turning into a serial killer, hunting down everyone he knew and loved?

He knew he'd have to go back into the house. That was inevitable. He could see it in the darkness now, casting its shadow, radiating its malevolence. Its brooding window-eyes searching for him, hungry for more victims. He knew the house was commanding Avril, ordering her to perform these atrocities, but he didn't have a clue why or how he was going to stop her.

His foot slipped on the slick grass.

He looked down. The weather had been dry for quite some time, so he knew whatever he had stepped in couldn't be water. It must be something else. His boots were black, so in the dark of the night, he couldn't tell if there were any stains on them or not, but he could see that whatever he had slipped in was thick and dark.

*Blood.*

He'd known it, he just refused to admit it. He didn't want to think about losing another friend. They'd been dropping like flies, and he was scared.

Tonight, was going to be the night it ended.

Tonight, was the night that he stopped … her.

He gripped the shaft of the hammer so tight it made his hands sweat. It was more for reassurance than anything else, as he once again had no clue what he was going to do with it if and when he confronted Avril.

With a determined breath, he ignored the gore on his boots and the relentless second guessing in his head and followed the trail towards the old house.

He scrambled through the bushes, careful not to touch the blood that was coating the leaves and branches around him. He understood that he was well within the clutches of whatever evil languished here. He could feel it prickling his skin as if some unseen force was tickling him, sizing him up as a potential victim, perhaps the last one it needed for whatever nefarious plan it was hatching to reach fruition.

Sucking on his cheeks, he gripped the hammer tightly and continued.

She'd taken them all now. All four of them, all dispatched in a similar manner. They'd been his friends; they had been *her* friends too.

Their friends.

Holding back, waiting until Avril, still dragging Heather, had entered the house, he pondered on the senseless loss, the violence, and the general weirdness of this night. He didn't have much time to dwell on it, though, as there was still much to do if he was going to stop Avril, and he was determined to stop her.

Quickening his pace, he made it to the old wooden steps. Careful enough not to make any excessive noise, he slowed as the shadow of the house engulfed him. The house wanted him there, it welcomed him. It had been expecting him, waiting. The door creaked as the wind blew it on its rusty hinges, as if inviting him, lulling him inside. There was a macabre sense of fun in the noise. Glee for the house, yet death, misery, and damnation for everyone else. He toyed with the idea of just turning around, of going home and pulling his blankets over his head and attempting to forget about this whole ordeal.

He knew it wouldn't happen; for some reason, he knew it couldn't happen, even if he'd really wanted it to. Things had gotten so far out of control, and someone had to bring this whole sorry mess to a gruesome conclusion.

A sad chuff escaped him as he thought about how it had all started. A stupid fucking *adventure!*

This time, things were going to be different.

*Why the fuck have I not gotten the police involved? This old Windsor place has really gotten under my skin.*

A cold chill ran down his spine as he thought about the basement, about the two bundles in his dream—or his waking nightmare, or whatever the fuck it was. When he thought about Avril unpacking them, seeing their hooded tops, his heart broke on seeing the different colours.

Joe and Flo.

Was all of this because of them?

Were they guiding Avril, forcing her to kill everyone who entered the house?

So much had happened in a strange timeline that it was playing with his head, adding to his sense of the unreal, confusion, and dread.

He didn't need a map or any clues to tell him where Avril was taking Heather. Everything that had happened, it had all been because of this old house and because of the basement beneath it. He wanted to burn the place to the ground. To smash up the old wooden furniture and burn every fucking thing out of existence.

With his anger affording him a steely resolve that kind of surprised him, he took in a deep, shaky breath and set his sights on the basement door.

~~~~

The night had a smell on the air that spoke of rain. It reminded Bradley of the smell when there had been a good run of hot, sticky days and the dark clouds began to gather, promising thunder and rain. It was musty but fresh at the same time. He knew this was kind of a paradox, but it was the best way he could describe it.

It heralded something coming to an end and a new whatever-that-may-be was on its way.
~~~~

It was an apt smell for what he was doing and where he was going, as after tonight, nothing would ever be the same again.

'*All these kids are going to die.*' The voice that had been plaguing him carried on the wind that was whipping around his head. '*All of them,*' it continued before morphing into a manic laugh that was difficult to listen to.

'Listen to them!'

Bradley stopped. That voice had been different. He recognised it.

It was Ted's voice.

'Listen to them, Bradley.'

That was Sam.

'Bradders, will you just listen to them?'

Chris.

Why was he hearing them now? Why were they urging him to listen to the horrible hissing in his head? They spurred him on. Maybe they were not dead. As this night had been replayed over and over, maybe he still had time to save them, to help them, to release them, as if this was all part of the *worst* horror movie he'd ever seen or even heard of.

'I'm coming,' he whispered, his voice lost on the wind and the night.

~~~~

He knew that to get to the bottom of what was happening, he needed to enter the creepy old place.

He was reminded again of stupid slasher/horror movies they'd loved to watch … him and Avril. 'Don't go into the house,' they'd shout at the TV screen. What he would give to be that person now, watching this shitty movie he'd found himself in and screaming at the TV screen.
~~~~

The door at the top of the old creaky steps was open.

It hadn't been closed from the last time he'd been here. *If I've ever been here*, he thought.

With a steely resolve, he continued up the steps.

Every one of them creaked.

Even in the cacophony of the blowing trees, the shutters, and the crazy wind, he could hear them. He knew whoever was in the house would be able to hear them too. He thought maybe even his mother and father, still in bed, possibly having nightmares about their son and an old house, could hear the creaks as he stepped gingerly towards his fate.

~~~~

The first thing he did once inside was turn on his flashlight. He'd remembered to bring it this time. It illuminated the musty hallway and the staircase that dominated it. He'd watched Chris and Sam disappear up that staircase twice. Looking to his left, he lit up the long corridor he'd seen Ted and Heather disappear down, neither of them really wanting to be there.

It was where he'd watched them die too.

He looked to the side of the staircase. The little white door, the one that Chris had denied was there, was hanging slightly ajar. *Built on rock, my ass*, he thought before heading towards it, following the bloody trail.

She was there.

Just inside, as he knew she would be.

'Bradley,' she whispered.

In his head, he heard Avril.

In reality, it was Heather. 'What are you doing here, Bradley?' she whispered.

'I've come for you,' he whispered, reaching his hand out. He noticed she was wearing the same shirt, jacket, and
~~~~

jeans that she'd worn on the night of the stay-over. *Last night, or tonight.* He couldn't think.

'Come for me? Why?'

'To get you to safety. Avril's gone crazy. She's got a knife and she's killing everyone. Ted, Sam, Chris. I thought I saw her stab you outside. Thank God you're all right.'

Bradley grabbed Heather by the hand and pulled her towards him.

Her legs didn't work.

None of her worked.

As he pulled, Heather's arm came away from her torso. It was then he realised that her touch had been so cold.

The scream that left him was unmerciful. Dropping the severed arm, he staggered back away from the human mannequin before him. With wide, petrified eyes, he stared at her dead, purple face with her dark blue lips.

Then the illusion fell.

It *had* been Avril's voice he'd heard.

With a wet sucking sound, the rest of Heather's body slipped to the floor. She'd been sliced into pieces and balanced back together.

'Hello, Bradley,' Avril said as she stepped through the human remains.

His flashlight caught the grin on her face. It was wide, too wide. Her expression didn't flinch as she stepped through what was left of their friend, treading on parts of her and grinding them into the ground like chuck fed to animals at the zoo.

The stink was atrocious, heavy, and wet.

Gone was the smell of the promise of rain, and here to stay was the smell of desecration, of mutilation, torture, and savagery. It smelt coppery.

'Avril. Wh—why? Why are you doing this?' He was stuttering because of the shock of what had just happened to Heather and because of fear, intense fear of the girl he'd wanted to be his girlfriend. It was also because the temperature had dropped twenty, maybe even thirty degrees. He was freezing. Avril, dressed in the same jeans and t-shirt she'd worn for the stay-over looked to be immune to the elements.

He looked down at himself. His clothing had changed. He was now wearing the same jacket and jeans he'd worn for the stay-over.

'Why what?' Avril asked.

'Why do this to everyone? They were our friends.'

For the first time, Avril's face changed. The smile faltered; she struggled with it for a moment before squinting as she looked at him. 'What are you talking about, Bradley?'

'Look at what you're …' He looked down at the floor, expecting to see the many parts of Heather scattered around his feet, but there was nothing there.

The gore was gone. The parts of Heather that had fallen apart right before Avril appeared were no longer there.

'What?' she asked, her feet dancing about as if trying not to stand in something invisible.

Bradley shook his head. 'I—'

'It's all good,' Avril interrupted. 'Come and see what I've found.' She reached for him, and he flinched.

'What's the matter? Weirdo …' She laughed. 'I wasn't trying to kiss you or anything. Come on.'

Bradley was confused. This was Avril. The same girl he'd spent night after night playing video games with and snuggling into on his bed while they watched scary movies. Not the crazed killer he'd feared since all this … shit had started.

She turned away and headed through the door, down the narrow staircase behind it. He saw her flashlight turn on.

For some reason, it calmed him, as he remembered the horrible feeling the last time he'd climbed down these stairs.

Holding his breath, he stepped through the doorway.

Nothing happened.

He stepped out again and then back in.

Again, nothing happened.

He shook his head and studied the frame with his flashlight. It was just an old frame made of wood that had seen much better days.

'Are you coming, or what?' Avril shouted from somewhere below.

He grinned. *Could it all have been some kind of whacked-out dream? A nightmare I've been trapped in, of my own making. Maybe my brain really does hate me, and it doesn't want me to get with Avril. It's been trying to villainise her or all this time.*

This thought was rational.

It was the only rational thought he remembered having for … he couldn't think how long.

'Coming,' he shouted back into the gloom.

He stepped through, and once again, nothing happened. With the weight of the world lifting from his shoulders, he took the steps two at a time into the darkness of the basement.

14.

IT WAS DARK where he was.

Although he didn't think he was tied up, his movements were restricted, and he couldn't see. His arms, his legs, and his lower back were screaming in agony. He needed to stretch, to work the muscles, to allow the blood circulation to make it back into his freezing extremities.

There was a noise like a shuffle or footsteps. Someone was coming. He had no idea who it could be.

He hoped it was Flo.

~~~~

</div>

She was in agony. Whatever or whoever had stuffed her into this bag was smothering her. She couldn't breathe, she couldn't move. The pain in her joints was unbearable; it was almost as bad as the agony in her chest, where she thought her lungs were attempting to implode.

She needed to breathe.

She wished she hadn't taken this bet, and they'd listened to the other kids, the ones who told her and Joe than no one had ever stayed over in this house.

Now, she knew why.
~~~~

15.

'WHAT DO YOU think is in them?' she asked, the glee on her features enhanced by the flashlight beam and the high pitch of her voice.

'I don't know. Maybe it's best just to leave them alone. You never know—'

'What if it's the remains of Joe and Flo?' She laughed spookily.

*That's exactly what I'm afraid of,* he thought. The smile on his face belied the angst he was feeling in his stomach. He shook his head. 'Don't mess with them. Leave them—'

Before he could finish, Avril had undone the first sack and was rummaging around inside it, her flashlight between her teeth. A line of drool was hanging from her open mouth, and Bradley watched as it dripped slowly onto the sack. *That can't be good,* he thought.

'Ugh!' she uttered, jumping back.

Bradley's heart was in his throat. He stepped back too, giving Avril space to move away from whatever it was she'd found.

'What is it?' he asked, not really wanting to know.

She took the flashlight out of her mouth. 'It's …' she paused, looking at the sack, wiping her hand, the one not carrying the flashlight, on her pants.

'It's what?'

She turned and looked at him, right into his beam. Her flesh, starched by the light, was pale. Her eyes were nothing but pinpricks, and there was snot dripping from her nose. Something had caught her eye behind him. Suddenly, he wanted to run. He wanted to drop everything and just get out of that basement, back into the clean air of whatever night it was out there now.

He'd had enough of this basement, this house, this whole scenario.

'*It's me,*' the hissing ancient voice rasped in his head. '*It's us!*'

~~~~

Suddenly, the house felt different. There was still a malevolence about it, but it no longer felt *old*. It was a strange feeling.

It was lighter too.

Bradley didn't need his flashlight, even though the room was still as dark as it had been. Everything shimmered a little brighter than it had done before. He spun around, looking for the owner of the voice. Us? It was a question he didn't want answered, although he had a feeling, he was going to get it anyway.

Yet there was no one there.

The basement was no longer there.

He found himself in the hallway, standing next to the old white door. It didn't look anywhere near as decayed as it had minutes earlier before Avril unravelled the bundles. It no longer had the ravages of age about it. Even the furniture scattered around looked newer, not exactly cleaner but like it hadn't been left abandoned to rot for as long.

He spun again, taking in a three-hundred-and-sixty-degree view of the room.

It was the same house, but not the same.
~~~~

None of this made any sense to him.

An odd feeling up his spine caused his flesh to cover in goosebumps.

Someone was watching him, laughing at him.

He held his breath, wondering why he always did that when he wanted to listen carefully. It wasn't like his breathing was overly loud or anything. There was laughing. It sounded faint, like it was far away, or at least in a different room, but it sounded young and full of life and mirth.

It sounded genuine.

It sounded at odds to the doom and gloom of the house, displaced, lost, like it belonged to another place, another time, *another when*!

Suddenly, footsteps thundered above him.

Someone was running around up there.

They were running and laughing.

*They?*

*Yes*, he answered himself. *They!*

The footsteps turned and thundered the other way. The laughter was young, like children having fun, maybe two of them. He put his hand on the banister and looked up the stairs. It was still pitch dark up there, but he could see perfectly. His eyes had gotten used to the gloom. A flashlight cut through the darkness, shaking up and down as if being held by someone running.

He tried to shy away, to hide from whoever it could be, but was too late; he'd been seen. It *was* a child running. He would have guessed they were no older than thirteen. It was a girl wearing a red hoodie. She was looking at Bradley, her flashlight pointing to the ground. If there had been mirth on her face moments ago, it was gone now.

Another thunder of running stopped abruptly, and a boy, roughly the same height and build with the same look, stared down the stairs at him. He was wearing a yellow hoodie.

Neither one of them spoke or even moved.

'Hello …' Bradley offered.

The newcomers turned to face each other before slowly looking back at him.

'Hey, my name is Bradley.'

'Bradley?' they asked together, their voices in tandem. There was a hissing aspect to the duality, reminding him of the voice he'd been hearing in his head.

He nodded, unsure if he would be able to speak.

Then, slowly, the pair took a step towards him.

He wanted to step back, wanting to maintain a safe distance between them, but was unable to move. The strange feeling that enveloped him on the staircase took hold again. It was as if he were covered in cottonwool or bubble wrap.

The two children took another step down the stairs towards him.

He could see them clearly now. They were nothing more than children, but they both had an age to them, as if they had lived—or existed—for years beyond their appearance. They also looked sad. Not scary or malevolent but like two scared school children.

'Bradley?' they asked again.

He nodded. 'Yes, I'm Bradley.'

'I'm Flo,' the little girl in the red hoodie said.

'And I'm Joe,' the boy countered.

'Are you here to relieve us?' Flo asked, cocking her head to one side as the question left her lips.

Bradley shook his head. 'No, I'm—'

The boy smiled. 'I'm so glad you've come. I'm so tired.'

'Me too,' Flo added.

'No, I'm not here to—'

'All these kids are going to die,' they both said together. Their voices hissed in the now familiar way, but something about it was different. It was no longer spooky. There was a tiredness about it but also an elated excitement.

'What?'

'They must,' the children replied. 'You don't want to walk these halls on your own.'

'Not for the length of time we have.'

'No, you've got it wrong. I'm not here to relieve you,' Bradley hissed, fighting the presence, or the force, or whatever it was holding him. 'We're just—'

'On a dare?' they asked.

'We were on a dare too. It was Halloween,' Flo said alone, her voice wistful and musical.

'We were new in town. We just wanted to fit in,' Joe continued. 'We took the dare because we wanted the kids to like us.'

'It was all in fun. Then we met someone.'

Bradley couldn't believe he was hearing this story. He didn't want to listen but found himself powerless against it.

'It was another set of twins,' Joe said, smiling a sweet smile.

'Just like us. They'd taken on a dare too, many, many years before. The house got them, you see,' Flo explained.

Bradley was shaking his head.

'When we found the two bundles, that was it for them. They'd served their time. They were able to move on because they'd found someone to replace them.'

'Us,' Joe concluded.

'No. This isn't right. This isn't true. I'm not here. You're not Joe and Flo. They don't exist; they're an urban legend, a story told to keep kids out of this place.'

They both nodded.

'This is true,' Flo replied. 'And it's worked. We've walked these halls for years, alone, with just each other for company. Now, you're here, you and all your friends. You're here to replace us.'

Joe produced a mass of burlap sacks. They were large enough to fit a body in. 'Now it's your time to get in the sack.'

His face had turned now. It didn't look evil as such, but it was serious even through the sadness in his eyes.

Bradley shook his head. 'No,' he muttered.

'It has to be. The house wants *you* now. It's had its fun with us. We are relieved.'

Flo put her hand on her brother's. 'Wait. He can't go into the sack just yet. *All* of these kids have to die.'

Joe nodded and dropped his hand. 'Yes. You're right.'

Bradley was suddenly free of the force around him. He relished the freedom and moved back as far from the creepy kids as he could get. He tried to shine his flashlight up towards them, just to keep an eye on where they were, but as he raised his hand, it was no longer holding a flashlight.

It was a knife.

It was the same knife Avril had killed the others with.

'What the ...'

'You must take the others. You must fill the sacks with their bodies. They are already dead; they just don't know it yet. They died the moment they entered this house. They were marked, and they were taken. All you need to do now is show them they are dead.'

Bradley shook his head. 'No, I can't ... I won't.'

'You have to.' A different voice entered the fray now. It sounded older than the twins' voices. 'You have no choice.'

Avril was standing beside him. Her neck was twisted in an impossible angle. Her eyes were yellowing, her skin pale, and her lips tinged purple.

'They're dead anyway. Just like I am, just like you are,' she said.

'No, I'm not. I'm still ...' Bradley protested.

Avril shook her head. It was horrible to watch, as her neck didn't work properly. 'No, you're not, Bradley. You're in a sack in the basement. The one next to mine.'

'I-I w-watched you,' Bradley stuttered. 'I watched you kill them all. It was fucking horrific.'

Avril grinned; she looked at him as if he were a child being spoken to by a teacher. 'You didn't watch me kill anyone. That was your dying brain synapses. You saw what your brain wanted you to see. You were dying, I was dying, and our friends were dying. You interpreted it as a cheesy horror film. The ones that we used to sit and watch for hours.'

He was shaking his head faster, more panicked now. 'No, I'm not. I'm not dead; you're not dead. They're not even real.' His voice had raised a few octaves as he pointed at the bemused twins. 'I don't know about you, but I'm getting the fuck out of this madhouse.'

'Bradley, you're not,' Flo said over his rantings. 'Your friend is right. You are already dead. The moment the spirit took you in the basement, on the steps. The tightness you felt was the sack. You were smothered, just like we were.'

'It's not true. Tell them, Avril.'

'It is true.' She nodded, her head wobbling at strange angles. 'I tripped and fell down the stairs. Then I was bundled into a sack, and when you came down after me, you were too. We're both in the basement right now. You've seen us.'

He opened his hand and dropped the knife. 'I won't do it. I won't kill my friends.'

'You don't have a choice.' Joe stepped closer to him; his face, while far from evil, was filled with impatience.

'He does,' Avril interrupted him, stepping forward and raising her hand to stop Joe's advance.

She looked at Bradley. Her neck was no longer at an odd angle. She looked as alive, as normal as he felt. A great sadness overcame him as she bent down and collected the knife he'd dropped.

'Don't,' Bradley whispered.

She looked at him with a smile on her face. It was melancholic, and it broke his heart. She shrugged. 'I have to. One of us does, and I don't want it to be you. I don't want you to be tarnished in any way by this. You're perfect and you're loving, Bradley. I've always loved you.'

He didn't expect tears, but they were running down his face at her little speech. There was no stopping them once they started either. 'Don't do it,' he sobbed.

Her eyes held his. There was love in them, deep love.

She blinked, just once. A single tear fell down her cheek.

Then she disappeared.

Bradley was left alone with the two ghostly children. They looked at him, their faces sadder than they'd been when he first saw them. He looked around, searching for the girl he'd watched do terrible things to their friends, the one who was about to do those terrible things again, just so he didn't have to.

'Why?'

Flo shrugged. 'We've done our time. It's our turn to cross over, just like the spirits who took us. We, like you, had no choice.'

'Your friends are already dead. They just need … convincing of the fact,' Joe said.

'But why does it need to happen like I saw it happen?'

'It won't,' Flo said with another sad smile. 'Look.'

Suddenly, everything around him changed. It shimmered like in a dream sequence in a movie. He was suddenly in another room in the house, the same room where he'd witnessed Avril kill Ted. He was by the window, looking towards the door. Avril was there too, standing just inside the door.

Ted ran in, laughing at someone outside. Bradley knew it was Heather. He stepped forwards, hoping to warn his friend about what was going to happen.

'You can't interfere,' Avril said, her face drawn and sad. 'It has to happen like this.'

Ted stopped when he got inside the room. He looked at Bradley and then Avril. 'What are you two doing in here?' he asked. The laugh dropped from his face as he eyed them both.

'Ted, you know the stories about Joe and Flo?' Avril asked.

Ted nodded.

'Well, they're true.'

She brought the knife from behind her back and showed it to him. He looked at the weapon, his face accepting of whatever was about to happen.

He looked at Bradley and then at Avril. 'Are you two …?'

'Dead?' Avril finished for him, nodding.

'Am I?' He was looking at Bradley.

It was his turn to nod.

'How?'

'I have to kill you, but I promise it won't hurt.'

'It won't hurt? Bro, you're about to full on kill me, and you're telling me it won't hurt.' Ted was laughing as he turned away from them. His shoulders slumped, and he looked over his shoulder at Avril brandishing the knife. 'Just do it quickly. Would you do that for me?'

Avril reached around him and brought the knife across Ted's neck.

'Promise you won't hurt me,' Ted said.

'It's already done,' Avril said, stepping away from him.

Ted faced them both. His neck was pouring blood, the cut so deep it looked like it had almost taken his head clean off. It was remarkable that it hadn't fallen. Avril pointed to Ted's feet. There was a large brown sack stuffed full of something resting there.

'Is that me?' he asked.

Avril nodded, then looked at Bradley. He nodded too.

Ted shrugged, then grinned.

The cut in his neck healed instantly. 'It is what it is, I suppose,' he said with a laugh.

Bradley and Avril looked at each other.

'Is he serious?' Bradley asked.

~~~~

The next thing they knew, they were at the top of the landing looking down onto the grand hallway below them. It was still dark, but they could see.

Sam and Chris were climbing the stairs, holding hands. Bradley watched them reach the top. Both of them ran through him as if he wasn't there—which, he supposed, to them, he wasn't. As they ran along the corridor, Chris was teasing her about something. It played out like a movie on mute.

Chris was pointing to the door, and Sam was shaking her head. He toyed with the handle, but she kept backing off. They played this game for a short while, each of them flirting with the other as if Chris wasn't gay, which was exactly how he acted with everyone.

'Fuck this,' Bradley said and pushed through Chris and opened the door.

Chris stepped back and looked at it. He pointed to it and then looked back at Sam, backing away from the room.

Avril looked at Bradley. 'This is no good. We need him in there and her out here alone.'

Bradley nodded. He stepped back from his mark and ran at Chris. He barged into the bigger youth, knocking him into the room. The door slammed closed behind them.
~~~~

Chris screamed like a girl as he fell forward, leaving Sam alone with Avril.

Sam turned, looking for someone to help her, someone to get Chris out of the room she didn't want to enter. 'Avril?' she said, shocked to see her standing behind her. 'I thought you were with Bradley.'

Avril grinned.

'Why are you smiling? That door just opened on its own and swallowed Chris!' She rushed every single word in the sentence, so it sounded to Avril like one long word. *'Thatdoorjustopenedonitsownandswallowedchris!'*

'We need to help him,' Sam pleaded.

'No,' Avril replied, deliberately slowly. 'We don't.'

'Yes, we do! God only knows what's happening in there.'

Avril offered her sometimes-friend a smile. It wasn't the most comfortable smile she'd ever cracked, but it was the best she could do in the situation. 'I know exactly what's happening in there,' she whispered.

'Stop being weird and help me open this door.'

Avril shook her head. The motion was slow and definite. 'You need to die now, Sam.'

Sam looked away from the door where Chris had disappeared, her wide eyes holding Avril's. Neither girl looked away.

'Right now?' she asked.

'Right now,' Avril said, nodding. She looked down at her hand and was not surprised to see she was holding the knife tight in her grip. Her hands were sweating, which she thought was odd, considering she was dead.

'Will it hurt?' Sam asked.

Avril gave her head a small shake.

Sam exhaled and looked away, on the verge of tears. It wasn't anything like the drama Avril thought she might start after being told she was about to die. She took it rather graciously.

'Why did we do this? Why didn't we listen to what everyone said about this fucking house?' Sam asked.

'I don't know. I feel bad because I talked Bradley into coming. So if you think about it, I killed him.'

'Ow! What the fuck, Bradley?' Sam shouted as he appeared from nowhere, banging into her. 'Why did you do that?'

'Do what?' he asked with a grin, standing next to Avril.

'Bang into me, dickwad.'

Bradley's grin widened. 'I didn't bang into you, Sam. Look down there.' He pointed to her feet.

Sam's eyes followed.

'Ew! What is that?' she asked, stepping away from the strange bundle that had appeared on the floor.

'That's you,' Avril replied.

She looked at it, then back at them. Her face was creased, and she looked disgusted. 'Me? I can't be seen running around the afterlife in a … in a sack!'

Avril chuffed. 'You really are a vain bitch, aren't you?'

Sam flashed a sardonic smile and offered her friend a middle finger.

'You can wear whatever you want to wear,' Bradley offered.

'Really?'

'Really,' Avril replied, dreading what the girl was going to end up in.

In an instant, Sam was dressed in a cheerleader outfit, her long, muscular legs accentuated by the short skirt and her boobs pushed up almost impossibly aided by the best push-up bra the afterlife could offer. 'Hmm,' she purred. 'I could get used to this.'

'We need to get in there and see Chris,' Avril said.

There was no reply from Bradley. She nudged him, and he flinched, as if remembering where he was. 'What?'

'Eyes front and centre, soldier,' Avril snapped. 'We need to go and kill Chris.'

'Can I come?' Sam offered.

'No,' they both replied, in unison.

'Fine. Damn, I only asked,' she sulked.

~~~~

The room was dark. There were no windows to speak of and, as far as Chris was concerned, not much of anything else.

He was rattling the doorknob, trying to get the door open so he could *get the fuck out of here!* Something he had never told anyone, for fear of his reputation going down the drain, was that he was scared of enclosed spaces and the dark. Truth be told, he was petrified of them. 'Sam, Sam, can you open this door, please?' he asked nicely, his voice hiding his rising panic. 'Sam, come on now. This isn't funny. Please just open the door and let me out. I, erm, I really need to take a leak. I'm about to burst in here.'

He rattled the knob again. 'Sam, open this fucking door!'

He kicked out at it, giving it a loud thump. 'SAM, OPEN THE FUCKING DOOR. I NEED TO PEE.'

'You don't need to pee.'

It was everything he never wanted to hear.

A disembodied voice coming from the darkness.

It was every nightmare he'd had from as far back as he could remember, from a young boy shaking under his blankets as he imagined his closet door swinging open on its own in the middle of the night. The irony of him being scared of something coming out of his closet was lost on him. He might have laughed, but he was far too fucking
~~~~

scared to do anything but open his bladder and let go of the pee he'd been lying about.

'Who the fuck's there? Show yourself, you pussy. Come out and fight me. Come on.'

'Chris, calm down, will you?'

'What? How do you know my name?'

Something hit him. It was a punch in the chest, and he fell back against the door he'd been rattling. It opened, just a little but enough for him to be able to see again. He grasped for the light like a drowning man might grasp at a floating plank. He pushed the door, opening it even wider, allowing more dim illumination inside.

He slid down onto his ass, gasping, gulping in the light as if it were water.

He looked up as Bradley stepped into the room.

'Bradders? What the hell? How did you get in here?'

Bradley offered the bigger youth his hand. 'The same way you got down there,' he replied, pulling him up.

Chris was rubbing his neck as he looked at his friend. 'Am I dead?' he asked.

Bradley pulled his lips down in a pout and clicked air between them. 'Yeah,' he said.

'When you banged into me?'

Bradley nodded.

'And this sack here. That's me in it, isn't it?'

'Right again.'

'Fuck,' Chris spat. 'Is there any chance of killing Sarik?'

Bradley shook his head, laughing.

'So, I'm stuck with you fucking dumbasses for all eternity?'

'Seems that way. Not much we can do about it, really.'

'Who else have you got?'

'Everyone, besides Heather.'

Chris laughed as he looked inside his sack. 'Good luck with that one.'

Bradley nodded before turning to see Avril standing at the doorway.

'She's gone,' Avril said.

~~~~

The door was open. Bradley couldn't remember if they'd left it open or if it just didn't close properly. He and Avril were on the threshold to the property, both of them looking out at the grounds, both of them wondering exactly the same thing. They were questioning whether they could venture out of the house to retrieve Heather, who was currently heading full pelt towards the chicken wire fence on the outskirts of the grounds.

Neither voiced their question, but they were both pondering on a cult classic movie they both loved. They'd watched it a million times and almost knew it word for word. It was about a couple who found themselves dead in their home, and a horrible couple from the city moved in and began changing the house around them. They had brought in a freelance bio-exorcist to help them get rid of the living pests. It was one of their favourite movies.

They were thinking about sandworms.

In the movie, the woman left the house, and she was almost eaten by sandworms.

*Would that happen to us?*

'You need to catch her and bring her back' a voice from behind him instructed. 'If she makes it to the edge of the property, then there'll be no hope of redemption for any of us.'

They turned to see Joe and Flo standing behind them, looking out at the same scene they were looking at.

The fleeing, screaming girl.
~~~~

'There's no way I'm going to be able to catch her before she makes that fence,' Bradley said, watching Heather run.

'You're thinking about it as if you're still alive,' Flo continued. 'Newsflash, you're not. In death, all you have to do is think about being over there, and you'll be over there. Just like you were able to knock your friend into the room.'

'By just thinking about it?'

Both twins nodded.

Bradley gave them a side-eye glance as if he didn't believe what they were saying. He closed his eyes—he didn't know why; it just seemed appropriate.

When he opened them again, he was at the fence at the end of the garden with Heather running towards him. When she saw him, her wide eyes grew even wider. She tried to stop hurtling towards him, but her momentum was too much. She pulled a comical face as she realised, she was not going to stop before running into him.

Bradley smiled and revealed the knife. He held it out before him and allowed what was left of physics that mattered to the undead to do the rest of the work.

As she continued forward, her eyes were drawn to the weapon, and she screamed. Bradley winced at the sound, wondering if anyone else could hear it. Then he thought of what time it was and what the odds of someone being around at this time were. Very slim, he concluded. Either way, he thought it prudent to shush her.

As she ran into him, the knife slid into her chest.

She was physically dead.

She just didn't know it yet.

She screamed even louder and thrashed at him. Her arms were flailing, her legs kicking. He found out that even as a ghost, getting a kick in the shins still hurt—a lot.

'Heather, calm down,' he urged, trying to hold on to her but also wary of getting another kick. 'Calm down, you're already dead.'

She must have understood what he said, as the fight in her dissolved instantly.

'Come on,' Bradley said, wrapping his arms around her. 'You're not alone. We're all with you.'

'I'm dead?' she asked, her voice heartbreakingly sweet. 'Am I really dead?'

'We all are. We shouldn't have come into this house.'

'How?'

'Joe and Flo. It's time for them to cross over. Now it's our turn to look after the house.'

'That's not fair,' she sobbed as she accepted Bradley's embrace.

He hugged her tightly. 'I know. We all had a lot we wanted to do.'

Still holding the sobbing girl in his arms, he escorted her back to the house. He looked up to see Avril following them.

He smiled at her, and she smiled back.

## 16.

ALL EIGHT KIDS were gathered in the main hallway of the grand house. Everyone was holding hands and hugging. Chris was laughing at something Ted had said, and Heather was shaking her head at Sam, who was preening in a large mirror. Somehow, her boobs had gotten even bigger since she found out she was dead.

Bradley and Avril were standing with Flo and Joe. 'Do you really have to leave right now?' Avril asked, the smile on her face melancholic.

'We've held this house for sixty years,' Flo said, nodding.

'Our parents never got to find out what happened to us. They died not knowing,' Joe continued.

'It's time we let them know we're safe,' Flo concluded. 'Goodbye, Avril; goodbye, Bradley. We're sorry to have to do this to you, but we know the house will be in good hands. We know you will give the kids a good scary story to keep them out until it's time for all of you to cross over.'

'How long will that be?' Bradley asked. 'Sam is already starting to get on my nerves.'

Flo and Joe laughed. They then took each other's hands and simply disappeared. There were no goodbyes or prolonged farewells. There wasn't even any advice on what to do and what not to do.

Avril put her arm around Bradley's shoulders as they looked at the others. 'I suppose it could be worse,' Avril said.

'How could it be any worse?' he asked.

'There's no TV. We're going to be stuck here forever with no crappy horror movies to watch.'

Bradley laughed. 'Yeah, well, I think I've had enough of all that horror stuff, for one lifetime, anyway.'

The pair of them laughed as they went to join their friends.

# EPILOGUE.

THE OLD WINDSOR place was haunted. All the kids knew it. The dilapidated old building was a throwback to a time when people built their own houses, back before everyone lived in community blocks. It had been a curiosity to the local children for a century.

There'd been tales told in the virtual reality hangouts where the kids congregated to programme scary tales to relive in their own virtual worlds. There'd been many digital mappings of the old house and countless virtual tours, but as far as anyone knew, no one had set foot in the place for a hundred years.

The stories of The Six, a group of friends who went in one Halloween night to explore and never, ever came back out again, were legend.

The police had been called and the place searched from top to bottom, but they found nothing. The official story was a serial killer who had been active in the area had laid low in the house, and the six kids played right into his hands. They were slaughtered, dismembered, eaten, and whatever remains left were taken with him when he left as grisly souvenirs.

The tales of strange noises coming from the house—screaming, laughing, running, doors slamming, always at the same time, around three in the morning—had become urban legends over the years.

There had been talk of razing the old place to the ground to make room for more housing to support the ever-growing population, but that had been shot down by the powerful historical commission. The need to preserve historical sites was deemed too important to the growth and learning of future generations.

It was this that attracted the gang of teens currently standing in the overgrown, fenced-off grounds of the old Windsor place. The four of them were cold, scared, and excited, all at the same time. Laser flashlights and VR goggles were at the ready while they performed infra-red scans, searching for anyone who might be alive inside, waiting for them, laying a trap, just like they did for The Six that went missing decades before.

'It's empty,' the tallest boy reported after his scan was completed.

'Well, except for a family of rats or something living in the basement. Look.' The girl showed her readout to the boy, where a faint red signal was indicating body heat below the structure.

He looked at it, and his brow creased. 'Is that showing a cellar?'

The other two, one boy and one girl, looked at the readout too. 'No way. This house doesn't have a cellar. It's built on solid rock. There's no way there could be a subterranean structure. Back in the days when this house was built, they didn't have the technology to cut into—'

'Well, it obviously does, doesn't it?' the fourth youth interrupted, much to the chagrin of the girl speaking. 'I don't care about rats. All I want is to get in there and meet a ghost. Who's with me?' he asked as he strode confidently towards the decaying steps and the wide-open front door.

The others shrugged as if to say, 'We might as well.'

They all entered, flashlights illuminating their way.

'This place is stunning,' the tall boy announced, his mouth wide open as he regarded the grandeur of the hallway.

'It stinks,' one of the girls announced. 'It's smells like someone took a shit on a three-week-dead homeless guy.'

Everyone laughed.

'What's this door?' asked the boy whose strides had brought them into the old house in the first place—to face their fears and, as it turned out, their fates.

'It's a door to the cellar,' the girl who thought it impossible for the structure to have a cellar said.

'I'm going down there; who's coming?' the tall boy asked, acting a lot braver than he felt.

~~~~

Unbeknown to the group, six pairs of eyes were on them. The eyes of youths not much older than them. The only difference was that these had been the same age for decades now, and it was time for them to hand over the baton to a new generation.

The house *must* be haunted, and this group was the perfect group to take over that mantle.

Bradley looked at Avril. Grinning, he held her hand and closed his eyes.

Ted, Sam, Chris, and Heather did the same.

~~~~

'Whoa, what the fuck are those over there?' the tall boy whispered just loud enough for the others to hear him.

Everyone turned to see what he was talking about.

'Never mind them; what was that on the stairs?' the girl asked. 'Did anyone else feel that?'

On the far wall of the empty room, there was a small shaft of light that half illuminated something leaning against the wall. The tall boy shone his light in that direction and revealed what the darkness had been keeping from them.

Everyone gathered around, all of them looking at what was within the thin beam of light.

Six large burlap sacks were bundled together against the wall. They looked full and covered in dirt, the dust and murk of decades.

'*All of these kids are going to die.*'

The tall boy turned to look at the others. 'What did you say?'

Everyone looked at him as if they didn't know what he was talking about.

125

DE McCluskey

## Author's Notes

So, here we are on another set of author's notes. This novella took me by surprise. I was asked to do it as part of a group project with five other authors. Chisto Healy, Kelvin V A Allison, Cat Voleur, Ayralea Lander, and myself, with excellent covers designed by Ruth Anna Evans.

We were given a character and the story had to be about them, and the only other remit was that character had to die.

Five independent novellas, and they could all be as different from each other as the authors wanted them to be, yet still be in the same group. They could also be as extreme as they needed to be, splatter, sex, violence, gore, and goop.

So, my idea for this story started off as a Halloween apocalypse kind of story, but even though I had the story completely worked out in my head, I just couldn't get the hook for it. I started it about fifteen times and was not happy with any of them. I even got to about ten thousand words with one of them. Next, I had an idea of a possessed Halloween costume. Once again, after four, maybe five false starts … the idea stalled, and again, I just couldn't find the hook for it.

Then this story came into my head.

In one of my earlier comics, *Interesting Tymes*, I wrote a story called "The Haunted House." The idea of this tale is a direct sequel to that short children's rhyming story (check it out on Amazon). The idea stuck, and it evolved. It's not a sequel where you need to read the original to find out what's happening, but if you really want to, then please check it out.

The only thing this lost in its evolution was that it went from being a total gore fest extreme horror to being a fifteen-rated horror/slasher style book. But in its defence, I think it suits Halloween better this way.

I love the old slasher films of the eighties (not so much the more recent ones), and I wanted to give it that kind of flavour. A call back to simpler horror tales.

So, as I did in *Mutant Superhero Zombie Killing Disco Cheerleaders from Outer Space (with Uzis)*, this is my homage to a genre ... and I sincerely hope everyone gets it.

All These Kids Are Going To Die.

Time for a big thank you session.

First and most importantly, a huge thank you to Lisa Lee Tone, my editor. She had read some of my worst and some of my best, and yet she's still there, giving me sage advice as always and making time to do over my ramblings.

Corrina Morse for being one of THE most supportive reviewers in the community.

Christo Healy for asking me to join in this project. Everyone in the Books of Horror Facebook page, everyone in the Splatterpunk Horror Readers group, and everyone in the Psychological Thriller Readers group too.

I've also got to thank Lauren Davies, my other half, for giving this the final proofread, and Kelly Rickard for being one of the most unsung heroes of the proof-reading community.

And lastly ... but not leastly (is that a word?), YOU, the readers. Thank you so much, with all my heart. As I always say, without you, my inane ramblings and jumbled up words wouldn't have an audience, so I mean every single word.

So, thank you for reading, and now please go and REVIEW … I'll love you forever, as will every other author!

Dave McCluskey
Liverpool
August 2023

# DE McCluskey's Bibliography

Check out my other works, all available from Amazon Kindle, or from www.dammaged.com

## As DE McCluskey


1. Doppelgänger
2. The Twelve
3. Three Days in the City
4. Wooden Heart
5. In The Mood for Murder (with Tony Bolland)
6. Z: A Love Story
7. Short Sharp Shocks
8. The Contract (with C William Giles)
9. CRACK
10. Butterflies
11. Zola
12. The Adventures of Mace Masoch: Hard Times on Planet L'Bido
13. Cravings
14. TimeRipper
15. The Grinkle Nonk
16. Mutant Superhero Zombie Killing Disco Cheerleaders from Outer Space (with Uzis)
17. Glimmer
18. The City of the Fireflies
19. The Throne of Glimm
20. DeathDay Presents
21. Guardian
22. The Special Stuff
23. The Boyfriend
24. Sing Sing Sing for Murder
25. Reboot: A Cosmic Horror

## <u>As Dave McCluskey</u>

1. Interesting Tymes
2. Interesting Tymes x 2
3. A Christmas Carol
4. Edward D'Ammage Presents: The Wedding
5. Olf (graphic novel)
6. A Seagull's Tale
7. Santa's Lost Boot
8. Olf (novel)